RAFAEL

BAYOU BROTHERHOOD PROTECTORS

BOOK FIVE

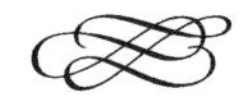

ELLE JAMES

TWISTED PAGE INC

ISBN EBOOK: 978-1-62695-524-0

ISBN PRINT: 978-1-62695-525-7

Dedicated to my readers who make my dreams come true by keeping me in the business I love dearly...WRITING! I love you all so much. Thank you for buying my books!

Elle James

AUTHOR'S NOTE

Enjoy other military books by Elle James

Bayou Brotherhood Protectors

Remy (#1)

Gerard (#2)

Lucas (#3)

Beau (#4)

Rafael (#5)

Valentin (#6)

Landry (#7)

Simon (#8)

Maurice (#9)

Jacques (#10)

Visit ellejames.com for more titles and release dates

Join her newsletter at

https://ellejames.com/contact/

RAFAEL

BAYOU BROTHERHOOD PROTECTORS
BOOK #5

New York Times & USA Today
Bestselling Author

ELLE JAMES

PROLOGUE

"Go! Go! Go! Lucky 7! You're the one. I just need you to make all my dreams come true!"

His heart pounded as fast as the horses' hooves on the track below. His twenty-dollar bet could be the one to beat all the bets that hadn't paid out.

If Lucky 7 won this race, he'd be the fifth winner he'd bet to win. The payout would be two hundred and fifty thousand dollars. Enough to pay off the loan sharks.

"Come on, Lucky 7! You can do it!"

The horses rounded the final bend and raced for the finish line.

Lucky 7, trailing by two at the corner, seemed to catch his second wind. He sailed past the chestnut, Don't Mind Me, and gained on the gray, Winchester's Metal, the favorite. At the very last second, Lucky 7 made one last push, sending his nose past the finish line a tenth of a second before the gray.

"I won! I won!" Suddenly, the ticket in his hand felt like something to be guarded, protected and clutched tightly until he made it all the way through the crowd and back to the teller to cash it in.

It was worth so much money that he carried it close to his chest, afraid the wind might blow it away or someone might come along and rip it out of his hand.

By the time he reached the teller window and handed in his winning ticket, his hands were damp with sweat, and he was one nerve short of a full-on panic attack.

He held his breath as the teller checked the ticket, then checked it again. She called for her supervisor and had him check it a third time.

The supervisor came out from behind the window. "Sir, could you come to the main cashier with me?"

"Sure, as long as it gets me my money," he said and followed the man to the track's main cashier.

After a couple more people checked his ticket, the manager of the cashiers approached him, stuck out his hand and said, "Congratulations, sir, you just won two-hundred and fifty thousand dollars."

An hour and a half later, he walked out of the racetrack with a bag full of money, nervously glancing over his shoulder, fully expecting to be mugged.

He made it to his car without incident and breathed a sigh of relief.

Now, where should he go?

Hit the loan sharks to pay back some of the money he owed?

If he paid off all his gambling loans, he wouldn't have anything left of his winnings.

He'd like to buy a new car.

With two hundred and fifty thousand dollars, he could start over someplace new. Someplace where no one knew him and the loan sharks couldn't find him.

The thought of keeping all the money for himself and starting over with a clean slate spread through him like warm whiskey. It warmed his insides and made him feel happy all over.

As he drove out of the parking lot, his cell phone rang. He glanced down at the caller ID and saw Cissy's name come up on the screen.

Happiness filling him to full, he answered the call. "Hey, beautiful. Feel like going out for a steak dinner tonight?"

"I don't know about that. Just heard from a little birdie you cashed in a big ticket at the horse track."

He frowned. "Word gets out fast."

"You know the Boss has eyes and ears everywhere there's gambling. He's gonna want his share for the loans you took out. If you're not planning on givin' it to him, you might wanna watch your back. I'd hate to see you fitted with cement overshoes and dropped in the bayou somewhere. Just sayin'—and you didn't hear it from me. See ya around."

His cell phone rang again. The caller ID was Jimmy Bangs, one of the many loan sharks he was sideways with. If he paid one, he'd have to pay all of them. They'd each want their share first and wouldn't be happy if he ran out of money before they got theirs.

His happiness sank into the pit of his belly. The idea of starting over seemed more like his only hope for survival now.

He checked in the rearview mirror. A minute later, he checked again. Was that black SUV following him?

At the next exit, he turned off the interstate and dove into a residential neighborhood where he wove in and out of the streets.

When he thought he'd lost the SUV, he took one of the smaller highways out of New Orleans, heading west, the bag of money on his seat feeling like a massive target for thieves and the New Orleans Mafia. He'd heard of guys who'd been dumped in the bayou for not paying off their loans. He'd been dodging collectors, trying to win back some of the money he'd lost, only to lose more and more and getting deeper into debt.

He'd passed the small town of Bayou Miste and

pushed on when another black SUV fell in behind him. Either way, if he stopped for food or gas or was run off the road, someone could easily knock him off and take the money.

He needed to put the money somewhere safe, where no one would think to find it. He could lay low until things quieted down, and he figured out where he could go to start his new life.

With the SUV on his tail, stashing the cash became his number one priority.

He passed the turn-off for Bayou Mambaloa and looked for a place to pull off the road. As he approached a series of curves in the road, he sped up instead of slowing down, taking the curves too fast for an SUV. A narrow gravel road turned off to the left with overhanging trees and overgrown vegetation along the sides.

He slammed on the brakes and drove onto the narrow, rutted road, going back far enough no one would see him from the road. He shut off his engine, rolled down the windows and listened for the roar of an SUV engine passing on the highway. When he was sure it had gone, he started his engine, turned around and headed back to Bayou Mambaloa.

After parking his car in an alley behind the businesses on Main Street, he looped the bag over his shoulder and went in search of a place where he could hide the money. An antique store caught his attention. They'd have furniture, maybe an old cabinet with a price so high it wouldn't sell in the next week or so until he could get back to collect his winnings.

As soon as he stepped through the door, he saw exactly the right place to stash the money. He waited until the man who ran the place was distracted. Then he stuffed the bag into a drawer. The problem was that anyone could open the cabinet, and they'd find the cash. He had to seal it.

Taking a chance, he left the bag of cash in the drawer, ran down to the hardware store and bought a tube of clear adhesive. He slipped it up his sleeve and walked back to the antique store. The owner was busy showing a customer every piece of hobnail glass in the store.

After checking that the bag was still there, he caulked the drawer edges, sealing it shut.

Cash on ice, he left the store and drove out of town, vowing to be back within a week. The thought of all that lovely cash made him smile until he remembered...he didn't have any of it in his pocket.

Well, damn. He couldn't go back to that town so soon. He'd just have to make do.

CHAPTER 1

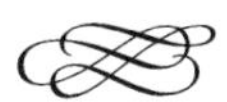

Rafael Romero elbowed Valentin Vachon in the side, nearly spilling the man's beer. "Don't drink so much you can't help me move tomorrow."

Valentin held the stadium cup full of the frothy liquid away from his shirt until the liquid quit sloshing. "Man, don't be poking a guy in the ribs when he's holding a full beverage. What are you worried about, anyway?" He tipped the cup back and drank it down to a more manageable level. "It's not like you have a lot of shit."

"No, I don't," Rafael agreed. "I just need help getting my bed out of the boarding house and up the stairs into my new place."

"Then why worry about how much I'm drinking?" Valentin asked.

Rafael lifted his chin toward the cup Valentin raised to his lips. "Can't have you still half-looped tomorrow morning and falling down the stairs. I haven't looked into rental insurance yet, especially the liability portion of it."

Valentin snorted. "Lighten up. This is my first beer of the evening and likely won't be my last." He tapped his toe to the beat of the music played by the band on the makeshift stage set up near the banks of the bayou. "What do they call this kind of music?"

"Zydeco." Their regional boss, Remy Montagne, pointed to the banner stretched across the street. "Like the sign."

"Oh, yeah," Valentin grimaced. "I knew that."

Remy's brow twisted. "How long have you been away from Louisiana?"

"Too long," Valentin said. "But then, I didn't live this close to the bayou or New Orleans. We didn't have Zydeco festivals in Monroe. Too far north. The people there are more like folks in southern Arkansas. Not as Cajun."

Gerard Guidry kicked an empty beer can. "Where'd you score an apartment?"

"Over the yoga studio." Rafael braced himself for the ribbing.

Landry Laurent snorted. "Next door to the Mamba Wamba Art and Gifts shop and the pretty shop owner he's been drooling over since we arrived in Bayou Mambaloa."

"Is she still giving you the cold shoulder?" Valentin asked.

Rafael cracked his knuckles. "It's only a matter of time until she succumbs to the Romero charm."

"And then what?" Gerard asked. "Never known you to go out with a woman more than twice before you leave her crying in her beer."

"The old hit-n-run routine, huh?" Valentin returned Rafael's elbow to the gut.

"This is a small town," Remy warned Rafael. "Folks don't take kindly to guys who do their women wrong."

Rafael's brow knitted. "I'm upfront with the ladies. I let them know I'm not into commitment. If that's what they're looking for, they might as well move on."

Remy's lips twisted. "I'm sure that goes over well."

"Every woman thinks she can change a man," Rafael said with a shrug.

"And your proof that they can't?" Valentin shook his head. "Are you sure you want to move in next door to her? What happens when you get her to fall for you, and then you bail on her?"

Rafael shrugged his shoulders. "I'll still have a great apartment over the Yoga studio."

Gerard frowned. "Next to the woman you wronged?"

Valentin raised a hand. "I call dibs on the apartment." He chuckled. "And the gift shop owner, for that matter."

"I think you're playing with fire," Lucas said.

Rafael cocked his head to one side. "How so?"

"You do realize Gisele is the granddaughter of Bayou Mambaloa's infamous voodoo queen," Beau reminded him. "If you're not careful, they'll put a spell on you and turn you into a poodle or a frog."

Rafael grinned. "You don't believe in that stuff, do you?"

"Damn right I do," Beau said. "Better to believe and keep my distance than not believe and eat flies with my tongue."

"Good point," Rafael said with a frown.

"Why don't you go for someone not connected with the local Voodoo queen?"

"Yeah," Lucas seconded. "Like the woman we saw you with at the Crawdad Hole the other night."

Rafael's brow furrowed. "Who?"

"The blonde you were all over." Gerard laughed. "Do you date so many you can't remember?"

"No. I don't date so many." Rafael shook his head. "You must be talking about Bianca. I wasn't all over her. She was all over me like an octopus. I bought her one drink, and she hasn't stopped bothering me since." He glanced over Remy's shoulder and swore.

Remy frowned. "What?" He started to turn.

"Don't move," Rafael said. "We have incoming." He stepped sideways, using Remy as a shield between him and the advancing blonde of their previous discussion.

"Oh, Remy, there you are," a feminine voice sounded behind Rafael. "Thanks for waiting for us."

Rafael spun to find Remy's fiancée, Shelby, advancing toward them, along with a gaggle of his teammates' womenfolk.

Shelby hooked Remy's arm. "Ready? We have to hurry if we want good seats for the show."

Remy gave Rafael a twisted grin. "Sorry, dude. You're on your own."

In less than two seconds, his teammates bailed on him, including the ones without women.

Completely exposed and unprotected, Rafael muttered, "So much for having my six."

Bianca Brolin rushed in for the kill. "Romeo, darlin', I just knew you'd come to the festival." She wrapped her arms around his neck and planted a loud kiss on his unresponsive lips. "We'll have so much fun spending the night together."

Already shaking his head, Rafael reached behind his neck to disengage her arms. "Excuse me, Bianca, but I'm with friends tonight. I'd better hurry if I want to catch up."

Before Rafael could step free of her tentacles, Bianca grinned, hooked one hand through his arm and covered it with the other, firmly locking them in place. "Perfect," Bianca said. "I'd love to spend more time with your friends and get to know them better."

"Uh, no." Rafael tried to pull his arm free. "My plans didn't involve a plus-one."

She smiled up at him. "See how things just fall into place? It's like magic. Me. You. The festival. It was meant to be." She looked around. "What do you want to do first? Eat mudbugs? Wrestle alligators or listen to the concert?"

He shook his head. "Don't you have some girlfriends to hang with? I'd planned on being with my team tonight."

She blinked up at him. "But they're gone. Now, it's just you and me. Don't you want to be with me? I mean, after the other night at the Crawdad Hole I thought we made a connection."

Rafael tugged again at the grip she had on his arm. Her fingers tightened, refusing to release their hold. "Look, Bianca, I'm sorry if I gave you the wrong impression."

"Not the wrong impression at all. Not after that kiss..." She drew in a deep breath and let it out with a sigh. "I could tell it meant more than just a one-time event. It's like love at first sight, or first kiss, in this case." She leaned into him. "I know you felt it, just like I did. I haven't stopped thinking about it. You must've had a busy week since you didn't call me."

Obviously, gentle and subtle wasn't working on the woman. Rafael peeled her fingers free of his arm and quickly stepped back. "Miss Brolin, I had a little too much beer that night. I never should've kissed you. I promise you I didn't feel anything."

"What?" Bianca's eyes widened. "But you had to

have felt something. No one kisses like that and doesn't mean it." She stepped toward him.

Rafael took another step backward. "Seriously, I felt nothing."

"Perhaps we should kiss again," she said, smiling tremulously. "Just so you know for sure. Your lips could've been numb from the beer. I'm sure a second kiss will prove that you really do have feelings for me. That you quite possibly love me as much as I love you."

"You just kissed me. Again," he stressed, "I felt nothing." Rafael glanced around. Where the hell was his backup? Why had they ducked out on him in his time of need?

Rafael gripped Bianca's arms before she could take one more step closer. "Miss Brolin, I don't love you. Never have and never will. Don't waste your time thinking there could be anything between us. There isn't. Now, if you'll excuse me, I want to rejoin my friends."

Her face fell, and tears welled in the young woman's blue eyes.

Rafael dropped his hold on her arms. "Oh, no, really?" he muttered. "We barely know each other. How could you possibly think we could fall in love over one dance, one kiss and one night in a bar?"

Bianca sniffed. "I knew as soon as I saw you that you were the one."

"I'm not the one for you, Miss Brolin," he said

softly. "I'm not the one for anyone. I'm not ever going to marry or fall in love."

Tears slipped down the blonde's cheeks. "I can change your mind. I just know it."

He shook his head. "You're not going to change my mind. No one is going to change my mind."

She stood with her arms at her sides, tears streaming down her cheeks.

Rafael felt like a heel, having made the woman cry. His natural inclination was to soothe her, to make her feel better. He also knew it would be a mistake and only encourage her to keep trying.

"Oh, Romeo," she cried.

Before he could stop her, she flung her arms around his neck and crashed her mouth over his.

"Bianca?" a woman's voice called out.

Rafael barely heard the sound as he fought off the woman with clinging arms like that of an octopus. The more he tried to disengage, the faster her hands moved to another part of his anatomy.

Finally, he grabbed her wrists and held them down. "This is crazy," he said. "What's it going to take to get through to you? I'm. Not. Interested. In. You."

"But I love you," she cried, twisting her arms in an attempt to free her wrists. "I know you love me."

"I don't love you," he said in a clear, precise way as if speaking to a child. "I never have loved you, and I never will."

A dark-haired woman rushed up to him and beat

at his arm with her fists. "Let go of my cousin. Do it *now*, or I'll call the sheriff."

Rafael immediately released Bianca's wrists and stepped back to find Gisele Gautier, the beautiful owner of the voodoo gift shop, glaring at him while pulling Bianca into a protective embrace. She was as dark as Bianca was light. How could the two women even be related?

Gisele's eyes flashed in their dark depths. "You're a beast to manhandle a woman like that."

"Manhandle…?" He stared at Gisele, grasping for a response to her outrageous accusation. "*She* wouldn't leave *me* alone," he protested.

"You expect me to believe that?" Gisele snorted. "You're twice her size."

"She's like an octo—" Rafael shook his head. "Never mind. Just keep her away from me."

"I loved him." Bianca burst into tears, sobbing loudly.

Passing people stopped, stared and frowned at Rafael.

"Oh, for crying out loud." No matter what he said, no one would believe him over a crying woman. He turned to the people standing around. "I didn't hurt her. I don't hurt women."

Several men crossed their arms over their chests and glared.

"I don't," Rafael insisted to no avail. "Fine. I'm leaving. Show's over." He stalked away, at first heading toward the boarding house he'd vacate the next morning. He'd be moving to the apartment next door to Bianca's cousin. The one woman in town he was even marginally interested in.

Oh, well. That ship had sailed.

At least he'd have an apartment of his own where he might get some peace and quiet so he could decide whether he would stay in Bayou Mambaloa with the Bayou Brotherhood Protectors or move on to someplace where the residents weren't crazy.

The thought of going back to the boarding house lost its appeal. The entire team was at the festival. He'd be damned if he let Bianca and Gisele shame him into leaving early. Hadn't he told Bianca he was spending the evening with his team? If he left now, it would appear to be an admission of guilt. Guilt over what?

He'd done nothing wrong.

Sometimes, his good looks were more of a curse than a blessing.

Instead of going back to the boarding house, Rafael marched through the crowd to the stands where his friends had found seats and were enjoying the music. He'd enjoy the music as well, even if it killed him.

GISELE SET her cousin at arm's length. "Did he hurt you? Did he break anything?"

Bianca sniffed loudly and rubbed her wrists. "He broke my heart," she said and started sobbing all over again. "I—" sniff "loved him."

Gisele pulled her close again, hugged her briefly and pushed her away again. "Well, he doesn't love you. Nor does he deserve you. You can find better."

"But I love him," Bianca sobbed. "I know if he'd just give me a chance, he'd see that he loves me, too."

"Honey." Gisele tipped her cousin's chin up, wondering how such a lovely girl could be so gullible and blind. "If he doesn't love you now, he won't love you even if he gives you the chance to make him fall in love with you. He's a heartless beast who needs to be taught a lesson in love."

Bianca blinked her pretty blue eyes. "Lesson?"

Gisele nodded. "A man shouldn't play with the emotions of a woman. What if he had the tables turned on them?"

"What do you mean?"

"What if a woman managed to make him fall in love with her and then dumped him like he dumped you?"

Bianca's brow knitted. "I don't want to make him fall in love with me so that I can dump him. I want him to love me like I love him."

Gisele sighed. "He's already told you he isn't interested. You'd be wasting your time. He shouldn't make a sweet young thing like you fall for him only to take advantage of you and then walk away when he's bored. What he needs is a little taste of his own medicine." Gisele's eyes narrowed. "I've a mind to give him a heaping dose of comeuppance."

Bianca touched her arm. "Gisele, that's not necessary. I wouldn't want him hurt or anything."

"Oh, I wouldn't hurt him physically. I'd just give him a taste of humility." Gisele tapped a finger to her chin.

Bianca's eyes widened. "Would you use a love potion on him? Because if you could get him to fall for you with a potion, why not let me have the option to use it on him?"

Gisele shook her head. "Potions only work where there's real potential for two people to fall in love. It helps them get out of their own way and be open to the other person. Too often, people come to me for love potions and then complain when they don't work. There has to be something there to begin with. Voodoo spells and charms aren't completely foolproof or magic. They just help enhance the magic inherent in each person to blossom and shine through."

"Have you ever had a potion fail to make someone fall in love?"

"Sadly, more often than you'd think," Gisele said. "And usually, it's because the person the purchaser is targeting isn't the least bit interested. They have no common ground on which to build a lasting relationship."

Bianca's pretty brow furrowed. "Then what good is a potion?"

"Exactly," Gisele said with a grin. "But don't tell my customers. That's where I make most of my money at the shop. People come in all the time for elixirs to improve their sex lives or make a boyfriend confess his love. I tell them that the potions don't always work, and there are no money-back guarantees."

Bianca brushed away her tears. "Without a potion, how can I get Romeo to fall in love with me?"

"You don't," Gisele said. "He was clear that he's not interested."

Her cousin cocked a brow. "Then how will you make him fall in love with you so you can dump him?"

"I'm not sure, but leave it to me. The man shouldn't get away with trampling on your or any other woman's feelings. He'll think twice before he treats a woman so cavalierly."

"I almost feel like I should warn him," Bianca said.

"If you do, how will I teach him that lesson?"

"It just doesn't feel right setting him up for a big fall."

"Isn't that what he did to you?" Gisele asked.

Bianca chewed on her bottom lip. "Well, yes...sort of."

Gisele gave her cousin a brief hug, "Then he

deserves the same." She slipped an arm around Bianca. "Do you need me to drive you home?"

Bianca shook her head. "No. I came with some of my girlfriends. I'll catch a ride with them."

"Then let me help you find them," Gisele hooked her cousin's arm. "I'd like to know you're safe before I leave."

"You're too good to me." Bianca leaned into Gisele. "I know you'll always look out for me."

"Yes, I will." Ever since Bianca's mother had committed suicide, Gisele had looked out for her younger cousin when her father had been unable to provide the feminine support the girl needed.

Bianca had an overwhelming need to be loved to the point of obsession. Gisele recognized it even if Bianca didn't. She'd tried to shield her from making huge mistakes with the wrong men.

Perhaps she'd done too good of a job at shielding to the detriment of Bianca's growth and maturity. Maybe it was time to just let the girl fall for the wrong guy and suffer the pain of rejection to its full extent.

Gisele couldn't. She was afraid her cousin would follow the same path as her mother and commit suicide rather than work through the pain.

She walked her younger cousin over to where her friends stood in a small group, talking and drinking beer while swaying to the zydeco music. After ensuring they would look out for Bianca, Gisele left the festival, walked back to her little shop on Main Street and started to climb the stairs up to the apartment over the shop only to stop, her brow furrowing.

The light over the back door wasn't shining as usual. She relied on that light to shed just enough light for her to see the steps up to her apartment. Had it burned out?

Gisele reached into her purse for the little can of mace she carried. Just because she lived in a small town didn't mean she was completely safe. Not a single woman alone at night. And the bayou was a great place to hide bad guys and bodies.

She shook her head at how quickly her thoughts turned morbid.

Holding the mace can out in front of her, her other hand went to the tiny ornamental gris-gris she wore around her neck. Her grand-mère, Bayou Mambaloa's resident Voodoo Queen, Madam Gautier, had fashioned the amulet of soft, colorful cloth and filled it with bits and pieces of items intended to protect her granddaughter. Gisele hoped it did the job.

As she inched toward the back door, she noticed it was slightly ajar.

The hairs on the back of her neck spiked. She started to back away when she heard a voice squawk, *Reach for the sky!*

A loud crash sounded inside the shop, immediately followed by the same squawking voice, *You break it, you buy it, asshole.*

Gisele gasped. "Johnny." She ran toward the slightly open door. As she reached out to push it open, a figure dressed all in black from the top of his head to his toes burst through it.

Before she could push the button on her mace, the man shoved her hard.

Gisele fell and landed on her back, the air knocked from her lungs.

CHAPTER 2

By the time Gisele caught her breath and rolled to her feet, the man was gone.

She staggered several steps and then ran into her shop. Once through the door, she slapped the light switch on the wall and stood for a moment, staring at the mess.

Candles and jars of lotions and tinctures littered the floor. The display shelf that had housed them had been toppled and lay in a splintered heap.

"Johnny?" Gisele held her breath.

Cheeky bastard.

Gisele released the breath she'd held in a rush of relief. She picked her way through the broken glass and slippery lotions to the giant cage lying on its side and the bright blue Macaw pacing back and forth inside.

You break it, you buy it, asshole, the bird repeated.

"Oh, Johnny." Gisele knelt beside the heavy cage, alarmed at the feathers splayed across the floor. "Are you all right?"

Get me a beer, woman, he demanded.

Gisele chuckled and shook her head. "No beer for you, big guy." She stood and tried to lift the cage off the ground, only managing to scoot it several inches.

Johnny flapped excitedly.

"I'm going to need some help." Gisele pulled her cell phone from her purse and called 911, her gaze on the back door she'd left open when she'd hurried in to rescue her parrot. She grabbed the broom she'd left leaning against the wall earlier and held it poised to strike if the man returned.

The dispatcher answered on the first ring. "Gisele? Is that you?"

Gisele recognized Minnie Hayes's voice immediately. Her south Louisiana drawl was warm and comforting after her nightmare encounter with an intruder.

"Minnie, someone just broke into my shop," she blurted.

"Oh, honey, is he still inside?" Minnie asked. "Are you somewhere safe?"

"I'm in the shop now. He's gone, but I need to report the break-in." Gisele stared down at the heavy cage and the macaw pacing inside. "And could you send someone over to help me? Someone strong?"

"A unit's already on its way," Minnie said. "Are you okay? Do I need to send an ambulance?"

"I'm fine, but the burglar knocked over Johnny's cage, and it's too heavy for me to lift."

"Poor Johnny," Minnie exclaimed. "Is he okay?"

Cheeky bastard, Johnny said.

Gisele's lips twisted. "As far as I can tell, he seems all right. I think he scared the burglar."

"Good for him," Minnie said. "Finally, his dislike of men came in handy."

"Right?" Gisele stared at the disgruntled bird, feeling sorry for the guy. His last owner had been a man who'd owned an antique store. Johnny had been orphaned when the man had a massive heart attack and died one morning before he'd unlocked the store for business. No one knew he'd died until three days later when a dealer came to deliver furniture the man had purchased.

Poor Johnny hadn't eaten since his owner had fed him the morning he'd died. Sheriff's deputies called the local veterinarian, Dr. Saulnier, to collect the bird to rehome him.

No one had wanted Johnny. His foul language and propensity to bite men had the veterinarian contemplating euthanasia for the feathered fowl.

Thankfully, Gisele had come to the vet's office to deliver a tincture she'd concocted for Linda, the receptionist, to help her have the confidence she needed to ask for a raise.

Johnny's cage was front and center with a sign posted next to it that read, *Adopt Me*.

As Gisele delivered her potion, the receptionist told her about Johnny's plight and the fact he'd be euthanized if he couldn't be rehomed.

When Gisele approached Johnny, he cursed but didn't bite.

She told the receptionist she'd take him if they could deliver him with the cage to her shop. She ran a few more errands that day. By the time she got back to her shop, a van was waiting to unload Johnny and his cage. He'd found a home, and Linda had gotten her raise.

Gisele had no problem adjusting to sharing her shop with the bird, but the customers proved more of a challenge. Tourists loved him, churchy women hated his potty mouth, and people became believers in the sign she'd posted that read, *I bite*.

So, he'd chased away a few customers.

Gisele couldn't have lived with herself if she'd walked away and learned he hadn't found a home and had to be put down.

Cheeky bastard, Johnny said.

"That's right. But he's a keeper," she said.

He's a keeper, Johnny echoed.

Gisele's eyes widened. She'd tried to introduce less colorful words for him to mimic. This was the first time he'd repeated anything she'd said. Up to that point, his vocabulary had been what he'd learned from his previous owner—all colorful and offensive to most people.

"He's a keeper," she said, hoping he'd repeat the words.

Johnny walked away. *Cheeky bastard.*

The sound of a siren made Gisele hurry to the front entrance. A sheriff's vehicle pulled up in front of her store, lights flashing.

The sheriff himself, Jimmy Bergeron, stepped out of the SUV and lifted his chin toward Gisele. "Ms. Gautier, I hear you ran into a little trouble."

"Yes, sir. Someone broke into the shop and made a mess."

As the sheriff started toward her, headlights flashed. Four vehicles raced along Main Street straight for the Mamba Wamba Gift Shop. The lead SUV had a rotating red light attached to the roof.

"What the hell?" The sheriff frowned, pushed his hat to the back of his head and stood fast while each vehicle came to a skidding stop around the sheriff and his ride.

The older man shook his head as the occupants leaped out. "I should write speeding tickets for every one of you." He lifted his chin toward Shelby Taylor. "Especially you, Deputy Taylor."

"I used my light," she protested. "Besides, when I heard my friend, a pillar of the community, was in trouble, I had to get here." She hurried forward and took Gisele's hands. "Are you okay?"

Gisele nodded, her gaze going to the man standing beside Remy, Shelby's fiancé.

Rafael.

Her pulse sped up for no reason. So, the man was drop-dead gorgeous. He was still a womanizer, breaking young girls' hearts. What was he doing there?

"Gisele?" Shelby's face moved in front of hers, blocking her view of the man whore.

Gisele forced a hint of a smile. "I'm fine. But the shop's a disaster, and I need help with Johnny."

"What's wrong with Johnny?" Shelby looked over Gisele's shoulder. "Did the perp hurt him?"

"Not that I can tell." Gisele stepped to the side, allowing Shelby to enter the shop. "He tipped the cage over, and I can't lift it on my own."

Shelby paused halfway through the door, turned and met Remy's gaze. "You hear that? A damsel in distress needs muscle power."

"On it," Remy said.

Gerard, the big guy on his left, cracked his knuckles. "Just show us where."

Before either man could move, Rafael was at the door, his big form sucking the air out of Gisele's lungs.

"The cage?" he asked, his voice deep and rich enough to make Gisele's mouth water.

Unable to form words, she nodded and moved

into the shop, hoping to put a little distance between her and the air-stealer.

As soon as he set foot in the shop, the space seemed to shrink tenfold, giving her no relief in breathable air.

When his teammates filed in behind him, Gisele stood with her back against a rack of voodoo dolls, trying not to get in the way.

As big as the men were, they gently lifted Johnny's cage and stood it upright. They'd just got it straight and in the spot it belonged when Remy jerked his hand back and cursed. He held up his bleeding thumb. "He bit me."

Cheeky bastard, Johnny said and flew up to his favorite perch.

The guys laughed.

"Might need this." Rafael scooped the *I bite* sign from the floor and handed it to Gisele.

She took it and grimaced. "Sorry, Remy. I have a first-aid kit beneath the counter." She started to step around Rafael to get it.

"No, don't bother," Remy said. "I'll take care of it at the house."

Shelby grinned. "I'll fix his boo-boo unless you'd rather I stay and help clean up."

"That's not necessary," Gisele said. "I can do it in the morning. I just needed help with Johnny's cage."

Shelby turned to the sheriff. "Do you want me to take her statement before I go?"

Sheriff Bergeron shook his head. "I'll take it. I have Jones on his way over to dust for prints."

Gisele shook her head. "The burglar was wearing gloves when he pushed me. I doubt he took them off while he was chucking things and nearly killing Johnny."

"If you're certain he was wearing gloves, I'll cancel Jones," the sheriff said.

Gisele touched a hand to her chest where her attacker had planted both hands and shoved her hard. "I'm certain."

Standing beside the sheriff, Rafael frowned. "Are you sure he didn't hurt you?"

Gisele rubbed her backside. "More my pride than anything. I should've doused him with mace, only he hit me so hard and fast I didn't have time to think."

Rafael's brow dipped lower.

"Do you have somewhere else to stay tonight?" the sheriff asked.

Gisele shook her head. "I live over my shop. He didn't break in there."

"But he could," the sheriff said.

"I think Johnny scared him off," Gisele said. "I doubt he'll be back."

"Are you willing to bet your life on that?" Rafael asked.

Gisele lifted her chin. "I have my mace and a can of wasp spray. I won't miss next time."

Felina Faivre pushed through the men. “Oh, Gisele, you can’t stay here. Come stay with me.”

Gisele’s heart squeezed in her chest. Felina was her friend, and they’d been roommates on several trips to New Orleans, but she was in a new relationship with her guy, Lucas. Gisele didn’t want to be a third wheel. “Thanks, Felina, but I’d rather stay here. I’ll be all right.”

“You could stay with us.” Bernie Bellamy, another one of her friends, hooked her arm through her man’s elbow. “We have a spare bedroom. Gerard and I would feel better if you weren’t alone tonight.”

Gisele smiled at the tall couple. Gerard the tallest of the team of men who called themselves the Bayou Brotherhood Protectors, stood several inches over six feet. Bernie was almost as tall at five feet ten.

“You’re too kind,” Gisele said. “But I need to be up early and ready for a shipment tomorrow morning. I’d rather be here.”

Shelby shook her head. “If you insist on staying in your own apartment, you need someone to stay with you.”

Rafael stepped forward. “I’ll stay.” His dark hair, dark eyes and incredibly handsome face were almost too much to resist.

Gisele’s breath caught and held for a moment. She could understand why Bianca had fallen for him so quickly. Her eyes narrowed. He had to know the effect he had on women and probably used it to his advantage to lure them into a giddy state, and then bam! One more notch to add to his bedpost.

Absolutely not.

"No, thank you," she said, a little more forcefully than she'd intended, especially if she followed through on her promise to Bianca to serve him a little taste of his own medicine. She might still do it. How satisfying would it be to make him fall for her and then ditch him like he had ditched Bianca? She had to do it.

Just not that night. After being knocked on her backside, her tailbone hurt, and she was sure she'd be stiff and achy the following day.

"I'll stay," another man stepped forward and held out his hand. "We've not formally met. I'm Valentin Vachon."

Out of habit, Gisele took his hand and gave it a brief shake before releasing it. "Nice to meet you."

Valentin gave her a half-bow. "I'd happily stay down here in the shop overnight to make sure your intruder doesn't return."

Reach for the sky, Johnny squawked behind Valentin

Valentin's hands shot into the air.

Laughter erupted from the other members of his team.

Valentin's cheeks flushed a ruddy red as he lowered his hands and turned to face the macaw. "Quite a bird you have there."

Gisele's lips twitched. "He speaks his mind."

"And bites," Remy said with a grin. "I advise maintaining your distance."

"Come on, big guy." Shelby hooked Remy's arm. "Let's get you home to some antiseptic and a bandage." She nodded toward Gisele. "Let one of the guys stay here tonight. They're protectors. That's what they do."

Gisele's brow dipped. "I can take care of myself."

"That's what I thought, too," Shelby said. "Until I couldn't. Remy helped me out of a tight spot. I might not have survived without him. If you don't let someone stay the night for yourself, do it for me. I'll sleep better knowing someone has your back." She paused at the door to the shop. "Please."

Gisele sighed. "Fine." She pointed to Valentin. "He can stay down here. Johnny needs more protection than I do."

"Just don't stick your finger in his cage," Remy said as Shelby shoved him through the door.

Rafael crossed his arms over his chest and stared down his nose at Valentin. "Aren't you supposed to be out before dawn to help Shelby's brother-in-law bring a new refrigerator unit up from New Orleans?"

Valentin grimaced. "Right. Maybe you could go with him instead of me?"

Rafael shook his head. "It's your friend he's buying that unit from, not mine."

"I could arrange to do it another day," Valentin suggested.

Alan Broussard's Country Store was the closest grocery store in a thirty-mile radius of Bayou Mambaloa.

"If my memory serves me right, Alan has a refrigerator unit that's been giving him fits. He needs a new one desperately." Gisele shook her head. "You need to help get that unit installed sooner rather than later."

Valentin sighed. "You're right." He clapped a hand on Rafael's shoulder. "Which leaves my man Romero as your second-best choice for protection through the night. Still, better than no one."

Rafael's lips twisted. "Thanks."

Outnumbered by well-intentioned friends and outmaneuvered by a handsome Lothario, Gisele gave up. "Okay. He can stay. For Johnny."

"Good. I'm glad that's settled." Bernie pushed her sleeves up her arms. "I don't know about the rest of you, but I can't just walk away when there's this big a mess to clean up. Where's your broom and mop?"

While the sheriff questioned Gisele and had her check her safe and jewelry cabinet, the men and women still there went to work cleaning.

Bernie and Felina swept the glass and damaged candles into piles.

Gerard and Lucas scooped the piles into a trash

bag and carried it out to the bin behind the shop. Valentin followed the sweeping crew with a mop, cleaning up the potions and lotions.

Rafael repaired the broken doorframe and tested the deadbolt. "This will have to do for tonight. You'll need a new lock. I'll stop by the hardware store and drop by to install the lock tomorrow."

"Thank you," Gisele said grudgingly. She didn't like being beholden to anyone—especially the man she had targeted for a lesson in humility.

After he fixed the back door, he gathered the broken pieces of the shelf unit. With a hammer and nails, he was able to put it back together almost as good as new.

Not only was he incredibly easy to look at, but he was also a talented handyman.

Double the trouble.

Gisele placed the items they'd salvaged on the shelf and stood back, overwhelmed by the outpouring of help from her friends. Tears pooled in her eyes. Other than the empty spots on the shelf, no one would guess the place had been broken into.

She turned to the men and women who'd come to her rescue and gave them a watery smile. "Thank you. That would've taken me half the morning to do all by myself."

Felina hugged her. "You'd do the same for me."

Bernie hugged Gisele next. "I'm just sorry this

happened to you. Hopefully, the sheriff will find the guy and lock him up."

"Hard to find a man without fingerprints or video surveillance footage," the sheriff said. "But we'll do our best." He tipped his hat. "I'll have Jones drive by several times through the night and keep an eye out for you."

"Thank you, Sheriff," Gisele said.

After the sheriff drove away, Gisele walked out the front door with the others.

"We'll be heading out as well," Bernie said. "If you need anything, don't hesitate to ask. We're here for you."

"That's right," Felina said. "Just a phone call away." She turned to Valentin. "Since Rafael is staying, we can give you a ride back to the boarding house."

Valentin nodded. "Thanks." As he passed Rafael, he bumped his shoulder into Rafael's and murmured something that sounded like, "You can thank me later." Over his shoulder, and a little louder, he called out, "Don't do anything I wouldn't do."

As taillights disappeared down Main Street, Gisele stood in the doorway of the Mamba Wamba Gift Shop, along with Rafael Romero, the last person in the world she wanted to be alone with after the night she'd had.

"Well, I'm going to call it a night," she announced and turned to reenter her shop.

"Hang on," the man said. "I want to get some things out of my truck."

She waited while he opened the back door of his pickup and dragged out a rolled-up sleeping bag and a gym bag.

Gisele frowned as he carried the items into the shop, imagining him using that sleeping bag with one of the victims of his charm. "Are you always this prepared?" she said, her tone dripping with sarcasm.

He nodded. "I keep a go bag in my truck at all times. It's a habit I picked up in my days as a Navy SEAL. We deployed often and with little notice. We never knew where we were going or how long we'd be there."

His response took some of the wind out of her self-righteous sails. That had to be hard on family life, which led to the next question that popped into her mind. "How does that work with married life?" She congratulated herself for the roundabout way of asking if he was or had been married.

His lips pressed into a thin line. "It doesn't." He marched past her into the shop, carrying the sleeping bag and gym bag.

So much for a straight answer to an indirect question.

"Well, I'll leave you to get comfortable with Johnny," Gisele said from her position at the front entrance. "Just lock the door behind me. I'll be upstairs if you need anything."

He dropped his belongings and hurried toward her.

Gisele stepped out, expecting him to lock the door behind her.

When he followed her outside, she turned a frown on him. "You need to lock the door from the inside."

"Are you going up to your apartment?" he asked, ignoring her comment.

Her frown deepened. "I am. Alone."

"I'll go first," he said and stepped past her.

He was halfway around the side of the building when she caught up with him.

Gisele hurried to beat him to the base of the steps, where she ducked in front of him and stared him down. "Where do you think you're going?" she demanded.

He cocked an eyebrow. "To clear your apartment before you go inside," he said as if that was the most logical thing to any moron.

"I don't need anyone to *clear* my apartment, whatever that means." She tipped her chin upward. "You're staying in the shop, not my apartment."

"I know. But a protector makes sure the space the protected is going into is free of danger, which means I need to go in first."

She didn't like the idea of Rafael entering her apartment. It seemed too...personal. Like he was invading her space and would leave a little of himself behind when he left—which was complete nonsense.

"I'll only be a moment. I mean, how long could it take to clear your apartment? I can't allow you to occupy the space until I know for sure your attacker is not inside, waiting for a second chance to harm you. Either I clear your apartment, or you can stay in the shop with me tonight."

She silently debated with herself. If she argued that she didn't need someone to "clear" her apartment, it would only delay the inevitable. He was pretty adamant that he wouldn't let her enter until he did the deed.

She let out a huff of a breath and stepped aside. "Fine. Clear my apartment."

As he darted past her and took the steps two at a time, she called out. "But don't touch anything."

He paused halfway up the steps. "You should go back into the shop and lock the door."

"The hell I will." She crossed her arms over her chest.

"Then at least stay close enough I can see you at all times." He came back down the stairs, grabbed her hand and led her to the top. "Stay."

"I'm not a dog."

"Stay, please?" he amended.

She frowned. "Better, but I'm still not a dog for you to train."

"Fair enough." He held out his hand. "Key?"

She dug in the crossbody purse looped over her shoulder and handed him the key to her place.

"Don't go anywhere," he said as he unlocked the door. Then he disappeared inside, switching on the lights as he moved through the few rooms.

Gisele tried to remember how she'd left her apartment that morning. Had she made the bed? What had she done with her sheer baby-blue nightie she'd slept in the night before? Had she left it on the bed, put it in the hamper or dropped it on the floor as she'd staggered into the bathroom for her shower that morning?

She was still worrying about the location of her nightgown when Rafael appeared.

"Find anything?" she asked.

"Just this." He held out his hand, the object of her concern dangling from his index finger.

She snatched it away. "I told you not to touch anything."

"I couldn't help it," he admitted. "I practically tripped over it."

That's where she'd dropped it. On the floor.

"No boogeymen?" she asked.

"None," he said.

"Goodnight." Gisele pushed past him, her breast brushing against his arms, sending a spark of electricity throughout her system, coiling at her core.

"I'll be right below you. Just yell if you want me to come up," he said.

"Trust me," she murmured. "I won't yell." She'd let

an attacker strangle her to death before she called out for help.

Gisele entered her apartment and slammed the door in Rafael's face.

Was that a chuckle she heard?

Whatever. She only had to put up with him for one night, and she'd be free of him. Gisele dropped her purse on the table by the door and tossed the sheer nightgown in the waste basket beside it. How could she look him in the eye, knowing he'd seen what she slept in? Not only had he seen the nightgown, but he'd touched it with his big, callused hands.

She stalked toward her bedroom, stopped and returned to the waste basket. Why toss her favorite nightgown just because a man had touched it? That would be ridiculous and wasteful.

After retrieving the skimpy garment from the otherwise empty basket, she raised it to her nose. Was the scent clinging to it that of Rafael's aftershave?

Gisele drew in a deep breath through her nostrils.

Maybe. Or her over-active hormones were imagining the scent she'd detected as she'd passed so close to him that her breast had brushed his arm.

Yeah, sweet, gullible Bianca hadn't stood a chance against the overpowering charisma of Rafael Romero. They didn't call him Romeo for nothing. He was truly hard to resist.

But he needed to come down a peg or two. No man should be so confident. Even if he had every right to be.

She'd love to be the one to bring him down. Then who would have the last chuckle?

CHAPTER 3

Rafael grinned as he descended the stairs and reentered the shop below Gisele's apartment. What had started out to be a disaster of an evening, beginning with his run-in with Bianca, had come full circle.

The break-in at the Mamba Wamba gave him a second chance to prove to Gisele he wasn't a bad guy out to deflower her pretty cousin. He just wasn't interested in the blonde. Not when Gisele showed more fire and gumption than any woman he'd ever met.

He liked that she was an independent business owner who could stand on her own. She didn't need a man in her life. She was just the kind of woman he preferred. A woman who wouldn't chase him down when he stopped calling. Someone who was fine on her own before they met and would be fine again when he ended their brief relationship.

Though he was glad for the opportunity to start over with her, he was concerned about the attack on the business and Gisele.

As he stared around at the shop, he wondered why someone would break into the place and not attempt to rob the safe or steal the jewelry.

Unless he was some religious zealot bent on destroying anything to do with Voodoo, considering it blasphemous and heathenistic. After all, they were in the south.

But why now? From what Rafael knew about the feisty gift shop owner, she'd owned the place for a few years. During that time, no one had broken in and destroyed her products like tonight.

He crossed to the shelf he'd kluged together and fingered a few of the bottles. One was marked LP9. Huh? As in Love Potion #9?

Rafael shook his head. He guessed some people needed a little help in that department. He could have used some of that on his fiancée the night before their wedding to keep her from running off with the maid of honor. Had she been given a love potion, she might not have left him standing at the alter the next day, looking foolish and pathetic in front of his family and friends.

No. If he had to use a potion, it wasn't meant to be. His marriage wasn't meant to be. Alison had been smart enough to do something to get her happily ever after. Had she stayed and married Rafael, they'd have been miserable and would have ended up divorced within a year, if not sooner.

Cheeky bastard, Johnny squawked.

Rafael raised a hand. "Guilty, I'm sure."

Cheeky bastard, Johnny repeated.

"Mouthy little dude, aren't you?"

The parrot flapped his wings and hopped from his high perch to a lower one. He leaned over and pecked at an empty food dish. *Get me a beer, woman.*

Rafael looked around the cage and then behind the service counter, searching for bird food and found a bag of seeds on a shelf in the broom closet. With a plastic scoop he found next to the bag, he dug into the seed.

Rafael carried the full scoop across the shop toward the birdcage.

As he neared Johnny, the bird flapped his wings in anticipation. *Get me a beer, woman.*

"It's not beer, but maybe some of this seed will do the trick." He stopped in front of the cage, worked the latch free and stuck his hand in, pouring the seed into the food dish while only spilling a few tiny bits.

As he pulled his hand out, a noise sounded at the front of the building.

He turned to find Gisele standing there with lettuce leaves and what looked like different fruits. "Well, I'll be damned," she murmured.

Rafael frowned. "What? Was the bird seed in the broom closet not for the parrot?"

She shook her head.

He stuck his hand back in the cage to retrieve the food dish.

"No," Gisele said, hurrying toward him. "You got the right food." She came to a stop beside Rafael as he pulled his hand out of the cage, "It's just that Johnny usually bites any man who puts his hand close to his cage—like he did tonight with Remy."

Rafael's eyebrows rose. "Oh, yeah. I forgot. He kept asking for a beer. I assumed he was hungry."

Gisele nodded. "He probably is. That's why I came back down with some fresh fruit and vegetables. The seed is all well and good, but he needs a more balanced diet." She shook her head again. "He didn't bite you?"

Rafael inspected his hand. "No. He didn't." He shrugged. "Must have been too hungry to bite the hand that was feeding him."

"From what the vet said, he bit his last owner's hand almost every time he fed him. Neither the vet nor his vet techs could get a hand in Johnny's cage without wearing gloves."

"Just call me lucky." He grinned and held up both hands. "And I still have all ten of my fingers and toes."

Gisele smiled at him for the first time ever. That one smile stole the air from his lungs and left him stunned for a full three seconds.

Her eyes flashed with amusement. "Valentin was so startled when Johnny exclaimed, *'Reach for the sky,'* I nearly lost it."

Rafael chuckled. "Your parrot has quite a vocabulary."

She snorted softly. "I didn't teach him the words or phrases he knows. His previous owner was a man who ran an antique store and liked to drink beer. Johnny came to me with those phrases. His language can be offensive to some."

"Not to you?" Rafael asked.

Gisele shrugged. "I've been known to bust out a curse now and then—usually, when I've stubbed my toe or broken something. Never to hurt anyone's feelings." She tipped her chin toward the birdcage. "Johnny doesn't know what he's saying." Her lips twitched. "Except when he asks for a beer. Apparently, his previous owner taught him that phrase to remind him that his food dish was empty." She pushed a piece of mango between the bars of the cage near the upper perch.

Johnny hopped up to the perch and went to work on the offering.

While he was occupied with the mango, Gisele opened the cage door and set the rest of the fruits and vegetables on the cage floor. Once she'd secured the door, she turned to the shelf Rafael had fixed. "Thanks for putting my shelf back together. I'll have to work on some replacement items to refill it."

"Are the bottles actual Voodoo potions?" Rafael asked., not ready for Gisele to leave.

Gisele's eyes narrowed. "Yes. Why do you ask? Do you need one?"

He held up his hands. "Not at all. I'm just curious. Who buys them? Do they get them as pranks or gag gifts? They don't really believe in magic, do they?"

Gisele lifted her chin. "Do you believe in magic, Mr. Romero?"

Rafael shook his head. "Of course not. Magic isn't real. It doesn't exist. You can't put your hands on it. Touch it. Feel it."

Gisele crossed her arms over her chest. "Do you breathe air, Mr. Romero?"

His brow twisted. "We all do," he said.

"Can you touch it or feel it?" Gisele asked.

Rafael frowned. "No."

"Neither can I," Gisele said. "Does it make any less real? Can we live without it?"

"No," Rafael said. "But that's different. We have to have oxygen to breathe and live."

"Just like magic, you can't feel it or touch it." She smiled. "But you believe it exists. Who is to say magic doesn't exist? Maybe all you need to do is believe that it exists."

Rafael's brow dipped lower. "How do you know if your potions work? Have you witnessed the effects your potions have on your customers?

She nodded. "I have."

"And do they work?" Rafael asked.

"For the most part." Gisele lifted one of the bottles from the shelf. "This mixture is one I concoct to help people with depression."

Rafael cocked an eyebrow. "Did it cure a customer's depression?"

"Not so much cured, but it helped that person to feel better about herself. I encouraged her to volunteer at the animal shelter. She swears the potion worked." Gisele's lips twisted. "I think the dog she adopted is the real reason she's no longer depressed."

"Remy tells me that people buy into your voodoo because your grandmother is the Bayou Voodoo Queen."

Gisele cocked an eyebrow. "And that doesn't scare you?"

"I find it fascinating."

"Not unnerving?"

He shook his head. "Not at all."

"You aren't afraid I'll put a hex on you and turn you into a cockroach?"

Rafael laughed. "You'd do that?"

Her narrowed. "If you hurt my cousin again, I might consider it."

His smile faded. "I don't know what your cousin told you, but I have no intention of having a relationship with her. Not now, or ever. I tried telling her several times, but she wouldn't let it go."

"You broke her heart," Gisele accused.

"I don't know how." Rafael shoved a hand through his hair. "I only danced with her once at the Crawdad Hole, and she thinks I'm in love with her. I'm not. I'm sorry if I hurt her feelings, but I'm not interested in her."

For a long moment, Gisele held his gaze as if assessing his words. Finally, she shrugged. "Bianca is young and impressionable—and she's beautiful. She's used to every guy falling all over themselves proclaiming their love. She could be confused. But I saw you two kiss."

"You saw *her* kiss *me*." He drew in a deep breath and let it out slowly. He hadn't been able to get through to Bianca. Now, he was having difficulty getting through to Gisele. "I'd like to put the entire incident behind me." He held up a hand like he was swearing on a witness stand. "I promise that I'm not going after your cousin. Though she is attractive, she's not my type." As soon as the words were out of his mouth, Rafael wished he hadn't said it.

Gisele lifted her chin and stared down her nose at him. "And what would your type be?"

He didn't speak at once, wanting to choose his words carefully. "I prefer a woman who is more mature and isn't clingy. Someone who knows who she is and what she wants out of life. A woman who doesn't need a man to define her. And she needs to be passionate."

Gisele snorted.

He stepped closer and cupped her cheek. "She needs to be passionate in her beliefs and in her love." He stared down at her face, falling into the depths of her eyes. "Passionate in her love," he repeated, "for her family, her community and animals. I couldn't be with a woman who didn't love animals or who didn't defend her family."

Gisele's tongue slipped out and swept across her lips, leaving a glistening sheen Rafael found hard to resist.

He wanted to kiss her. To claim those lips and taste this woman who'd been more concerned about her bird than her own life. One who'd come to her cousin's defense when she'd thought she was being mistreated.

He's a keeper, Johnny squawked, pulling Rafael out of the trance he'd fallen into.

He straightened, let his hand fall to his side and gave Gisele a tight smile. "I'll walk you to your door."

"That's not—" she squeaked, cleared her throat and started again. "That's not necessary. Good night, Romeo—er...Rafael." She spun and darted for the front entrance.

He's a keeper, Johnny repeated as she ducked through the door.

Rafael grinned at the bird. "Thanks for the vote of confidence." He followed Gisele out the door and to the base of the steps leading up to her home above the shop.

She ran up the steps and dove into her apartment, slamming the door shut behind her.

Rafael climbed up after her. When he reached the top, he tapped his knuckles against the door. "Gisele?"

"Go away," she said, her voice sounding as if she stood immediately on the other side of the door, not halfway across the room inside.

"I really need to check your apartment for intruders."

"There's no one here but me," she said. "Go away."

He shook his head even though he knew she couldn't see him. "Not until I'm positive you're not being held hostage and being forced to say what you think I want to hear."

"I'm not being held hostage," she said.

"Prove it," he insisted.

The sound of locks turning was followed by Gisele yanking open the door. "See? It's just me."

"Have you checked in your closet or under your bed?" he asked.

"Oh, for the love of—" She stepped aside. "Check for yourself."

He entered and made a quick pass, thoroughly checking behind, beneath and inside places a person could hide. When he was satisfied, he returned to where Gisele stood at the door.

"All clear," he said. Before she could make a biting

retort, he cupped the back of her head and dropped a light kiss on her lips. "Sleep tight."

Then he was out the door, pulling it closed behind him. He paused on the landing, listening. "Lock the door."

The sharp metal click left him with a smile on his face.

He hadn't planned on kissing her. But he'd kissed her anyway.

And she hadn't slapped him.

His grin broadened.

If she'd been angry about the kiss, she wouldn't have hesitated to slap him into tomorrow.

She hadn't slapped him. Which meant she was either too shocked by the move or was still recovering from that shock.

Or she'd like the kiss.

Rafael chose to believe the last scenario. He let himself back into the shop and locked the door behind him.

As he passed Johnny's cage, the bird fluffed his feathers and gave him the side-eye. *Cheeky bastard.*

Rafael laughed out loud. "Damn right, I am. And I have no regrets."

He'd chosen the apartment over the yoga studio next door to Gisele's shop with the express purpose of getting to know the woman better.

So far, it was proving to be a great idea.

He unrolled his sleeping bag and flipped the light switch, plunging the shop into darkness.

In the little bit of light shining through the front window from the streetlights on Main Street, he found his sleeping bag and laid down on top of it. With his hands laced behind his head, he stared up at the ceiling. If he was correct, her bed was directly over him.

He wondered if she was thinking about that kiss. He sure as hell was. The way her lips had felt against his only made him want to kiss them more.

He'd have no trouble staying alert through the night, not when his body was on fire for the woman so near and yet so far.

He'd have to work hard to win her over to go on a date with him.

But he was up for the challenge as long as she wasn't looking for anything long-term.

Although...

He shook his head.

No.

Short relationships only.

He never wanted to stand at an altar again.

Been there, done that and had the scars to prove it.

CHAPTER 4

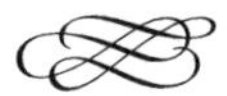

AFTER THAT UNEXPECTED KISS, Gisele tossed and turned in her bed until she gave up at three-thirty in the morning and got up. If she wasn't going to sleep, she might as well get to work on making more of the potions and lotions she'd lost in the break-in.

For the next three hours, she worked over her stove and kitchen table, stirring ingredients and murmuring incantations—her goal: to keep too busy to think about the man sleeping on the floor below her. No matter how hard she tried to banish him from her thoughts, she couldn't help treading lightly to avoid alerting him to the fact she was awake. He couldn't know how disturbed she was by that kiss.

She tried to tell herself he was playing right into her plan to make him fall in love with her so that she could teach him a lesson about love and humility.

Only the more she dwelled on that kiss, the more

she realized how dangerous it would be to spend too much time in his presence.

She could see how Bianca, a more impressionable young woman, could fall so completely and so quickly for Rafael. The man was entirely too handsome and practically oozed sensuality by simply breathing.

She'd be a fool to carry through with her plan. When the sun came up, she'd send him on his way. She wouldn't have to spend another night with him in the same building, running the risk of a repeat of that brief and potent kiss.

That kiss...

Heat rushed through her, coiling at her core.

Why?

He probably hadn't given it a second thought and was sleeping like a baby while she'd been awake all night.

Cheeky bastard.

Speaking of cheeky bastards, why had Johnny refrained from biting Rafael when he'd been true to his nature and taken a chunk out of Remy's finger?

Was Rafael a parrot whisperer as well as a fifth-degree black-belted womanizer?

She paused mid-stir of a new batch of Motion Lotion designed to ease stiff, arthritic joints in her elderly customers like Donna LaDue. What had she just added to the recipe?

Focus.

She needed to get the ingredients right or she'd end up sending sexual stimulation lotion home with old lady LaDue.

Damn.

Because she couldn't remember what she'd put in the pot, she dumped the whole batch down the drain and started over. What a waste of time and ingredients.

When she added each ingredient, she made a note on a piece of paper, forcing her mind to remain on task until the last item had been added.

Gisele made it through the batch of Motion Lotion and moved on to LP#9.

She'd lost half a dozen bottles of this product in the break-in. She sold a lot of Lip Plump #9 to the ladies. They loved it and swore it helped give them fuller and plumper lips.

By the time the sun appeared, Gisele had a dozen bottles of LP#9 and Motion Lotion lined up on her kitchen table. She'd have to make a visit soon to her grand-mère's place on the bayou for more of the secret ingredients she used in both items.

Tired, but ready to begin the day, Gisele ducked into the shower for a quick rinse, then spent time taming her long black hair into a neat bun at the nape of her neck. She took a little more time than usual with her make-up. Not to impress Rafael, she told herself. More to bolster her confidence for when she thanked him and escorted him to the door.

Soon, he'd be out of her shop and out of her life.

She should have been happy at that thought, but she wasn't.

"He's a ladies' man. You don't have time for his kind of nonsense," she muttered as she left her apartment and descended the stairs.

Her hand was poised with the key to the shop when the door opened, and Rafael greeted her with a smile, a cup of coffee and a bag that smelled like fresh donuts. "Thought you could use some sustenance since you were up at three-thirty."

So much for treading lightly.

She stared at the mug and the bag.

"Cinnamon latte with an extra dash of milk," he said waving the cup under her nose. "And the bag contains a chocolate éclair. Both are from the Bayou Bakery."

Gisele frowned. "How—"

"I didn't leave if that's what you're thinking," he said. "Shelby called on her way to her early morning shift and asked if I wanted anything from the bakery. I gave her my order and asked her to pick up your usual."

Her frown deepened. "You know my usual? What are you? Some kind of stalker?"

He laughed. "No. I jog in the early morning and saw you leave the bakery one morning with a coffee and a bag just like this. It's a small town. I figured the woman who ran the bakery would know what you liked."

"Amelia," Gisele nodded. "I don't even have to order. She knows what I like." She looked up into Rafael's face. Moments earlier, she'd been intent on showing him the door. To do so now would be rude. "Thank you." She took the coffee and the bag from his outstretched hands and carried them to the back of the store where she had a worktable and two chairs.

He could stay until she'd consumed at least half the cup of legal stimulant. Then she'd walk him to the door.

He followed her and held one of the chairs as she sank into it. Then he dropped into the other, wrapped his hand around another insulated cup of coffee and nodded toward a half-eaten jelly-filled donut. "They make the best jelly-filled donuts."

Gisele pulled the éclair out of the bag and inhaled its rich fragrance. "Amelia trained in France. She can make some of the most beautiful French pastries."

"Why isn't she working in New York or New Orleans?"

"Instead of being stuck in a backwater town like Bayou Mambaloa?" Gisele sipped her coffee and closed her eyes as the warm liquid flowed down her throat and all the way into her belly. "She came here from New Orleans. Rumor has it she had a bad breakup or a run-in with another chef." She picked up the éclair. "New Orleans' loss and our gain." Gisele took a bite from the éclair, glad to chew the sweet pastry. With a mouthful, she wouldn't be expected to keep up the conversation. Which was a good thing, because the only thing she could think to say was to ask him why he'd kissed her.

"I was thinking..." Rafael cradled his coffee cup. "And maybe the sheriff already asked you... Is there anyone you've angered recently? Someone who might be carrying a grudge?"

She shrugged. "Not that I can think of."

"A competing business wanting yours to fail?"

"I'm the only store in town selling remedies and voodoo tchotchkes." She took another bite of her éclair.

"Are there any self-righteous mamas on a mission to eliminate Voodoo from the bayou?"

Gisele shook her head and swallowed. "No. I give free samples of my facial moisturizer to the PTA mamas. They love me and buy my products."

"Has anyone been the target of a Voodoo doll stabbing?" he persisted.

"Not that I know of. I usually only sell those to tourists. I had a run on them the past few days since the Zydeco Festival began. No locals bought them."

"Maybe someone from out of town?"

"Maybe." She sighed and sipped her coffee.

"Could it be someone who might have been the unwilling object of a Voodoo spell or elixir?" he asked. “Have you sold one of your remedies that could be used on someone the purchaser might target for revenge?”

“I don’t sell harmful remedies or elixirs—only things that can help people,” Gisele said. “No spells or black magic. I leave those to Madame Gautier, the Voodoo Queen. I dabble. She’s the expert.”

“Could someone have a grudge against your family based on something your grandmother might have done?”

“I don’t know. She hasn’t cursed anyone since Lester Faulkner tried to poison Tante Mimi’s malti-poo.”

Rafael’s eyebrows rose into the wisp of dark hair that fell over his forehead. “She cursed him?”

Gisele’s lips twisted in a wry grin. “He had the worst case of jock itch for over a month. He stayed away from the malti-poo and Tante Mimi after that.”

“How did she give him the jock itch?” Rafael asked.

She shot him a glance. “I told you; she invoked a Voodoo curse.” Gisele shook her head. “Oh, right. You don’t believe in magic.”

“Whether I believe or not, I take it Lester believed.”

“He did. And he didn’t like having jock itch for that long. When he promised to stay away from Tanti Mimi and her dog, Madame Gautier removed the curse.”

"How long ago did this happen?"

Gisele closed her eyes, trying to remember. "Fourteen years ago."

Rafael's brow dipped. "Has he caused you or your family any problems since then?"

"No. Anyway, it couldn't have been him last night."

"Why do you say that?"

"I'm five feet tall," she said. "Lester is about as tall as you. The man who broke into my shop wasn't nearly as tall as you. He was somewhere in between my height and yours."

"Are you sure it was a man?" Rafael asked.

Now that he posed the question, she wasn't sure at all. "I assumed it was a man because he was dressed all in black and wore black gloves and a ski mask. And he hit me hard, coming out of the shop. Hard enough to knock me on my ass."

"Close your eyes and think back to last night." Rafael leaned toward her.

Her pulse quickened at his nearness. Gisele closed her eyes to keep from staring into his. Even with her eyes closed, she was hyper-aware of the man. So much so that she could feel the heat of his body.

"Can you picture him?" Rafael's voice was soft and low.

Her breath caught and held. She forced her mind back to that moment when she'd reached for the door handle on the back door of the shop. She let the memory roll forward like a video in slow motion. "He came through the door so fast, it's a blur in my mind."

"Was there something in the way he moved that made you assume he was a man?"

She shook her head slowly. "It happened so fast. I was standing there. He rushed through the door, planted both hands on my chest and shoved hard. I landed flat on my back with the wind knocked out of me."

"Did you see him running away?"

Gisele tried to see him, but she couldn't. "No," she said, opening her eyes. "I was stunned and couldn't catch my breath. I have no reason to believe he was a man, other than he attacked me fast and hard. I couldn't imagine it being a woman." She sighed. "Great. That doesn't narrow down the potential suspects at all." She pushed aside the now lukewarm coffee. "It doesn't matter. I doubt he'll come back. It was probably an out-of-towner here for the festival who figured everyone would be there. A crime of opportunity. He wasn't counting on anyone leaving the concert early."

"And he wasn't counting on a mouthy bird," Rafael said with a grin.

His smile and the light twinkling in his eyes made Gisele's heart flutter. She pushed to her feet, abandoning her coffee and éclair. "I'm sure he won't be back. Johnny scared him enough to chase him off for good." She drew in a breath and took the next step. "No one would be brazen enough to attack in broad daylight. That being the case, you don't need to stay. My assistant will be here soon. Thanks for staying last night."

Rafael pushed his feet, his brow furrowed. "He could come back."

"And risk being seen?" She shook her head. "Too many people. Again, thank you for staying." She gathered his coffee cup, stuffed the half-eaten donut into a bag and handed both items to the man.

Rafael's lips twisted. "Trying to get rid of me?"

"I do have a business to run," she said. "The building is barely big enough for customers to wander through."

"And I would be in the way," Rafael finished for her and set the coffee and donut bag back on the table. "I should stay at least until your assistant arrives."

The front door squeaked open, and a young woman wearing jeans and a graphic T-shirt entered with a backpack slung over one shoulder.

Gisele turned and gave a relieved smile to her twenty-year-old shop assistant. "And there she is." She turned to Rafael. "This is Lena, my shop assistant. Lena, meet Rafael. He was just leaving."

Lena's brow furrowed as she crossed the shop.

Rafael stuck out a hand. "Nice to meet you, Lena."

The younger woman adjusted the backpack and then gripped Rafael's hand. "Nice to meet you, sir."

"Please, call me Rafael," he said. "Sir, makes me sound old."

Lena's cheeks flushed a soft pink. "Nice to meet you, Rafael."

Something unfamiliar stabbed at Gisele's chest. If she didn't know better, she'd suspect jealousy.

Rafael had Lena blushing. The man could charm the panties off any female with just a smile.

Gisele hooked his arm. "Like I was saying, he was just leaving." Without wasting any more time, Gisele marched him toward the entrance.

He didn't let her get far before he dug in his heels. "Wait."

"For what?" she demanded. The sooner he was out, the sooner her life could return to normal.

His lips twitched. "My sleeping bag and gym bag. Unless you want to keep them here for when I come back tonight."

"Not necessary." She dove for the sleeping bag he'd rolled and stuck behind the counter.

Rafael bent beside her and hooked the straps of the gym bag.

As they both straightened, Gisele's breath froze in her lungs. He was standing so close she could feel the heat radiating off his body.

He leaned closer, a light dancing in his eyes. "Did your sleepless night and your desire to push me out the door have anything to do with the kiss?" he whispered.

Her eyes widened, and heat rose up her chest and neck, filling her cheeks. "Not at all," she lied. "I'd all but forgotten it." She shoved the sleeping bag toward him in an attempt to insert distance between them.

It didn't work.

Because he was so much taller than her, he easily leaned over until his mouth hovered close to hers. He reached around the bag she held like a shield, cupped her cheek and winked. "I couldn't stop thinking about it either."

Mesmerized by his gaze and how close her lips were to his, she waited, anticipating another kiss like the one from last night.

Instead of a kiss, Rafael brushed his thumb across her bottom lip. "I left my phone number on the counter. Call me if you need me. I'll come at once. Otherwise, I'll see you later." He took the sleeping bag and gym bag and walked out of the shop.

For a long moment after Rafael left, Gisele continued to stare at the door, willing her pulse to slow and the butterflies storming the inside of her belly to calm.

"Wow." Lena came to stand beside her, her gaze on the door as well. "Where have you been hiding your hottie?"

Gisele frowned. "He's not my hottie."

"Seriously?" Lena's eyes narrowed. "Do you think he would go for a younger woman?"

Gisele's lips pressed into a tight line. "Probably. But you don't want to get mixed up with a man like that. He's a player."

Lena shrugged. "So? I gotta lose my virginity sooner or later." She waggled her eyebrows. "I bet he could teach me everything I need to know about sex."

Gisele gasped. "Lena!"

Her assistant chuckled. "I'm just yanking your chain."

Gisele let out a relieved sigh.

Lena's lips curled into a wicked smile. "I'm not a virgin." She ducked out of reach of Gisele's hand, reaching out to slap her arm. "I called it. He *is* your hottie."

"He's not mine," Gisele protested.

"Maybe not yet. But you want him."

Appalled at Lena's observation, Gisele asked, "Why do you say that?"

"Girl, it's written all over your face."

Gisele clapped her hands to her cheeks. "Is it that obvious?" she asked before she could think better.

Lena nodded. "Clearly." She grinned. "The good news is he's totally into you. He practically devoured you with his eyes."

Gisele snorted. "You've been reading too many of those werewolf romances. This discussion is over. We have work to do. I need you to take a box up to my apartment and bring down the bottles on my kitchen table."

Lena retrieved a box from behind the counter and headed out the front door with a smirky grin. "You hate it when I'm right."

"You're not right," Gisele called after the girl.

Lena's laughter faded as the door slowly closed behind her.

Gisele pressed her hands to her still-burning cheeks. "I don't want Rafael Romero. I don't want *any* man." Especially him.

She lifted her chin, reminding herself she was a successful businesswoman and didn't need a man in her life. They were entirely too much work for very little benefit.

But when he'd brushed his thumb across her lip moments before and kissed her last night, she was reminded of what was missing in her well-ordered life.

"Sex," she said aloud. How long had it been since she'd gotten laid?

Obviously, too long.

Her body immediately heated at the thought of having sex with Rafael Romero. What kind of lover would he be?

A good one.

She knew, without a doubt, he'd be really good.

All the more reason to steer clear of the man. If

she had sex with him, she'd be ruined for any other man.

He's a keeper, Johnny squawked.

Gisele turned to the parrot and sighed. "You're wrong."

As convinced as she was that he would be an incredible lover, she knew the man wouldn't stay.

Her best course of action, where Rafael Romero was concerned, was to stay as far away from him as she could get.

She had no reason to swing by the boarding house where he lived, and he certainly didn't need to buy souvenirs from her shop.

Avoiding him should be a piece of cake.

CHAPTER 5

GISELE AND LENA spent the morning arranging the new bottles of lotions on the shelf and unpacking the delivery that came not long after Rafael left.

By the time she officially opened the shop to the public, they had everything in place and the excess inventory stored in the back.

Lena flipped the sign in the door from CLOSED to OPEN and stood staring through the window for a long moment. "What's going on at the yoga studio?" she asked without turning around.

"I don't know." Gisele paused from wiping the dust off a display and glanced up. "Why do you ask?"

"There's a line of women standing in the alley, and there's a truck with a big mattress in the back. Oh, wait. A couple of big guys are lifting the mattress out of the truck. They're carrying it to the back of the yoga studio."

"Did she rent the apartment over the studio?" Gisele crossed to stand beside Lena.

She recognized one of the men carrying the mattress as the man who'd introduced himself to her at the festival the previous night. What had he said his name was?

Oh yeah.

Valentin.

Was he moving into the apartment over the studio?

All she could see of the other guy was pantlegs and shoes; the rest of him was hidden behind the mattress. They carried the king-sized mattress down the alley between the Mamba Wamba and YaYa's Yoga Studio, passing a gauntlet of middle-aged women in yoga leggings.

After the two men disappeared around the back of the building, the women fanned their faces and laughed.

Lena shook her head. "Crazy. A bunch of married women drooling over a couple of younger guys."

"They're married. Not dead," Gisele said. "The guy on the back of that mattress is friends with the one you met this morning. From what Shelby told me, that entire group of guys are prior military and easy on the eye."

"Yeah. I guess I get it. Just because the ladies are old doesn't make them immune. Your Rafael made my heart beat a little faster."

"He's not my Rafael," Gisele protested.

"Whatever. Having one of them in the neighborhood could raise property values." Lena cocked an eyebrow and looked down at Gisele. "Do you want me to ask YaYa which one moved in?"

Gisele shook her head. "No. I have a package that belongs to YaYa that the delivery guy left with me by accident. I need to take it over."

"I could do that for you," Lena offered.

"Thanks, but I have some business I want to discuss with YaYa," Gisele handed Lena the rag she'd been using. "You can finish dusting the upper shelves I couldn't reach."

Lena sighed. "Ask if the new guy is into younger chicks. I'm pretty mature for my age."

Gisele shook her head. "When are you going back to college?"

"Not until next month." The twenty-year-old gave her a bright smile. "But if you need me to stay, I can skip a semester."

"No way," Gisele said. "You're within a handful of semesters of finishing your degree. Then you can get out of the bayou and see the world."

"What if I don't want to see the world?" Lena stared out the window. "What if I like it here in Bayou Mambaloa and never want to leave?"

"You need to get away and sample what the world has to offer. Then, when you come back, you'll have something to compare with." Gisele shook her head.

"Besides, there aren't too many jobs available for young people."

"I could work here at your store. I'll have my accounting degree. I could keep your books and do your taxes while helping you in the store."

"Or you could start your own accounting firm," Gisele suggested. "After you've worked for another accounting firm in a bigger town."

"What if I don't want to be an accountant?" Lena asked.

Gisele gave the girl her full attention. "Are you having second thoughts about your degree?"

Lena shrugged. "Maybe."

"It's a good career to go into. People always need accountants."

Lena's lips pressed into a tight line. "But what if I get tired of it?"

"Have you thought of taking a minor in something different but still related, like financial or business management?" Gisele suggested. "What about supply chain management or statistical analysis?"

"I've thought of all of that. The problem is that I don't know what I want." Her gaze remained on the view outside the window.

"Then take an internship somewhere that sparks your interest. Give it a chance. See if you like the work. That will also give you something on your resume."

"You're a successful business owner," Lena turned

to Gisele. "How did you know you wanted to own and operate a gift shop?"

Gisele turned to the window. "I didn't want to be stuck for my entire life in Bayou Mambaloa."

"What?" Lena shook her head. "You didn't want to stay here? I thought you loved it here."

"I do," Gisele gave her a crooked smile. "But I needed to get away and see what was out there. I wanted to go somewhere I wasn't defined by my family. I wanted to be just me. Not the Voodoo Queen's granddaughter where people expected me to be all into magic and woo-woo stuff."

"But you're amazing. People come from all around for your lotions and potions."

"I only dabble. Madame Gautier is the expert. I never wanted to learn her secrets. I went to college, got a degree in finance and moved to New York City, where I worked for a big firm on Wall Street. Talk about an eye-opener. I went from being a medium-sized fish in a little pond—the bayou—to being a tiny fish in a huge pond filled with every kind of fish imaginable, including piranha and sharks."

Lena winced. "Was it bad?"

"At first, it was exciting." Gisele smiled at the memories of her first years in the big city. "I met a lot of people, had celebrity sightings in Manhattan and took vacations to Europe. I was free to be me. It was wonderful. I even fell in love with a co-worker."

"That sounds amazing." Lena's brow dipped. "I sense there's a but coming."

Gisele snorted softly. "On Wall Street, if you're not moving up, you become obsolete and are swept aside. I worked hard and absorbed as much as I could about everything to do with money. But it never seemed to be enough."

"What happened?"

"After the rosy glow of a new life wore off, I began to see the dark side of the industry and learned why they called it the rat race. People stepped on others to move up the chain. Ethics were for poor-minded weaklings. I didn't like who I was becoming."

"I can't imagine you as anything other than focused, kind and generous."

"I was focused all right, but kind and generous I was not."

"No way," Lena protested.

"Way," Gisele said with a grimace. "When I finally got a backbone and refused to do what I knew would make my grand-mère slap me into the next year, my mentors dropped me and moved on to the next gullible up-and-coming analyst. That person stepped on me as he moved up the corporate ladder, leaving me in a black hole like an untouchable. I was black-balled from within the company I worked for. My career was over there."

"Wow." Lena looked out the same window as

Gisele. "Couldn't you go to work for another company?"

"Once you're blackballed on Wall Street, you're toxic. I sent out hundreds of resumes." She shook her head. "Nothing. Not even a kiss my ass."

"Is that when you came back to Bayou Mambaloa?" Lena asked.

Gisele shook her head. "I refused to leave New York City with my tail between my legs. I didn't do anything wrong."

"But you didn't have a job," Lena said. "What did you do?"

"I did what I do best." Gisele's lips curved upward. "I became an independent day trader, buying and selling stocks, determined to prove to those bastards I didn't need them. Once I had a sizable portfolio that was generating a good flow of money, I bought a rundown shop on Main Street, sight unseen, packed my bags and left on my terms. No regrets."

Lena's lips twisted. "Well, aren't you just a ray of sunshine? Here you are telling me to go swim with the sharks. What? Don't you like me?"

Gisele chuckled. "Sounds all gloom and doom, but it wasn't. I got to travel, to live in a vibrant city and learn the business. But most of all, I got to know myself and what was important to me."

"Sounds like a lot of effort just to end up back here. I could skip all that and stay right here."

"I had to leave and almost lose myself to find the

real me. Had I stayed in Bayou Mambaloa, I might've come to the same conclusion, but it would've taken a lot longer for me to realize I've been who I am all along. As hard a lesson as it was, I wouldn't do anything differently. There are worse things I could be than the Voodoo Queen's granddaughter. At least I could hold up my head and be proud."

Lena's lips twisted. "I'm still not convinced that leaving home is what I want or need."

Gisele patted her arm. "You have time. Finish your degree, start a career and know you aren't stuck in that field for the rest of your life like the silent generation was. You're free to change directions. But start somewhere. Get out and live."

"I'll think about it," Lena said.

"And I'll go pay a visit to YaYa."

"Lucky," Lena muttered. "I might have to sign up for one of her yoga sessions just so I can get a glimpse of her new tenant."

Gisele collected the package the delivery man had left with her by mistake and crossed the alley to duck between the women still standing around, waiting for the men to pass through yet again.

The slim and fit forty-five-year-old YaYa, dressed in her signature yoga pants and sports bra, stood with a middle-aged woman who was busily scribbling information onto a form attached to a clipboard. When the woman was done, she handed YaYa the clipboard and a personal check.

"See you tomorrow morning at the seven o'clock session," YaYa said. "You're lucky. You were the last one I could add to that time slot. It's now full."

"My friend who lives close to the old boarding house told me that your new tenant jogs every morning about that time." The woman, probably in her fifties, leaned closer to YaYa and added, "And he jogs shirtless."

"I like to think you're coming to the morning session, not just to watch a man jog by without a shirt. You should come to yoga to improve your overall health."

"Oh, but I am," the woman said. "Every time that luscious hunk of a man jogs by, my heart rate will increase and fill my system with endorphins. The yoga is a plus. See you in the morning."

The woman sailed off to join her friends lining the alley as a couple more men carried boxes from the truck around the corner of the building.

Gisele recognized Remy and Gerard.

"I've heard of goat yoga." Gisele's lips quirked. "Is there a new trend in alley yoga?"

YaYa shook her head. "When news got out that I'd rented my upstairs apartment to the guy who jogs from the boarding house through town and back, women started showing up from all over town and some from neighboring communities."

Gisele laughed. "All because you rented your upstairs apartment to a man?"

"Yes. I know it sounds crazy." She tipped her chin toward the ladies lining the alley. "They arrived at the same time as the truck. I told them that they'd have to sign up for yoga if they wanted to stand around the building. Needless to say, I've had a steady stream of women signing up for the early morning yoga class."

"How did they know what time the truck would arrive and that you'd rented the apartment?"

YaYa gave her a conspiratorial wink. "I might have let it slip on social media to Bayou Mambaloa's biggest gossip."

"You amaze me," Gisele said with a grin. "Which one of the Brotherhood Protectors did you rent the apartment to?" She turned to find Valentin coming toward her, followed by another man. Valentin blocked her view of the other man's face.

"I rented the apartment to the best-looking one of the lot." YaYa's chest puffed out proudly.

The man behind Valentin came into view.

"Rafael Romero," YaYa said at the same time as Gisele mouthed the same name.

Rafael spotted her and grinned. "Hello, neighbor."

Gisele muttered a curse under her breath.

"Every time I look at him, my breath catches and my heart hammers hard in my chest. I feel like a teenager." YaYa laughed. "I'm as bad as all these ladies who will now be my early morning class. I've never met a man who gets my blood humming so quickly. Do you think he'd go for an older, more experienced woman? One with a flat ass, spider veins and crow's feet?"

"I'm sure he doesn't discriminate based on age or body type." After all, he'd kissed Gisele, gone after Bianca and probably half the women in the Parrish. He was one hundred percent a womanizer.

And he was moving in next door to her.

How the hell was she going to avoid him when he would be there every time she walked out her door?

To make matters worse, YaYa waved him over. "Rafael, have you met my neighbor, Gisele, the owner of Mamba Wamba?"

Gisele took his hand, shook it briefly and let go like it was a scalding hot baked potato fresh out of the oven. "We've met," she said, her tone flat.

"I spent the night at her place last night," he announced.

YaYa's eyes widened. "I was away in New Orleans last night at a ballroom dance competition. I didn't get home until the early hours of the morning. Pray tell. What did I miss?"

"Nothing," Gisele blurted.

"Everything," Rafael said at the same time. "Her shop was broken into, and she was attacked."

YaYa's eyes grew bigger. "Seriously? I've been so busy registering new clients I haven't caught up on the local news." She gripped Gisele's hands. "Are you all right?"

"I'm fine."

"Did he take anything?" YaYa asked. "You do lock up your cash in a safe, don't you?"

"No, he didn't take anything that I could tell," Gisele said. "And, yes, I lock up my cash in the safe. He tipped over a shelf of products and Johnny's cage. I think Johnny scared him off."

"Oh, sweetie," YaYa squeezed her hands, "I'm so sorry." She turned to Rafael. "And you stayed with her all night to make sure she was safe?"

"I did," Rafael said with a nod.

"In the shop. On the floor," Gisele clarified. "I slept in my apartment upstairs."

YaYa looked from Gisele to Rafael and back. "Such a missed opportunity," YaYa murmured. "But I'm glad you weren't harmed. What's this world coming to? Why would someone break into a voodoo gift shop? It's not like you're hiding a bag full of money or diamonds in there. Or are you?"

Gisele shook her head. "Just lotions, potions and cheap voodoo dolls and figurines. The most valuable thing in my shop is Johnny."

"No one is going to steal that bird," YaYa said. "He's too mean."

"I'm just glad he wasn't hurt when the intruder knocked his cage over," Gisele said.

"Did you notify the sheriff?" YaYa asked.

Gisele nodded. "I did."

"Was he able to find your burglar?" YaYa snorted and answered her own question. "Probably not.

Unless you catch him red-handed with his hand in the cash, you're out of luck. Even then, if he's got a good lawyer, they'd get him off, claiming his client was sure the cash was there for the taking." She crossed her arms over her chest. "You need to install a security system with video surveillance and alarms."

"I never thought anyone would want to break into my store." Gisele sighed. "It's not like it's a jewelry shop with diamonds and gold. Besides, it was probably someone here for the Zydeco festival. I'm sure Johnny scared him enough that he won't be back."

YaYa frowned. "I still think you need that security system. I'd have one installed here, but I don't have anything to steal but yoga pants, matts and refreshing drinks. And I don't live above my shop. So, if someone breaks into my shop I'm not at risk. They can take whatever they want. That's what insurance is for." She grinned. "But now that Mr. Hot and Dangerous lives above the studio, I think I'm set. I'm sure no burglar in his right mind would tempt the beast." She winked at Rafael.

Rafael gave his landlord a serious nod. "I'll sleep with one eye open."

"The good thing is that the window in the studio apartment overlooks your shop and apartment." YaYa pointed to a window on the second floor.

Gisele had never paid attention to the apartment over the yoga studio. No one had occupied the apartment in the three years since she'd lived there. YaYa had a cottage on the bayou and preferred to keep business and home life separate.

The window in the neighboring apartment hadn't been an issue. Gisele studied it now. It was directly across from the window to her bedroom. If she left her blinds up, he could look right into her bedroom.

"Isn't that convenient?" YaYa smiled. "Until you get that security system installed, Rafael can keep an eye on your place as well as mine."

Gisele swallowed hard, refusing to look at Rafael's grinning countenance.

What fresh hell had she landed in?

CHAPTER 6

RAFAEL ALMOST LAUGHED at the play of emotions on Gisele's face when YaYa pointed out the window in his apartment that faced the window in hers. The window in his new digs was in his bedroom. Having been through her place now twice, he knew exactly which window faced his.

Also, her bedroom.

His groin tightened. Not that she'd leave the blinds open while she undressed or anything. But knowing she was close enough he could throw a rock and easily hit her building stirred his blood more than he cared to admit, especially to her.

He recognized panic as the final emotion that flitted across her face before she schooled it into a mask a professional poker player would be proud of.

As far as he was concerned, her panic was good.

For him.

She'd practically thrown him out of her shop that morning after he'd teased her with the promise of a kiss and brushed his thumb across her lip instead. That move must have made an impression on her.

His jubilance sobered slightly.

Unless she viewed his attention as sexual harassment and was afraid he'd push his advances on her even more aggressively now that he was living across from her.

The last thing he wanted was to make Gisele afraid of him or uncomfortable in his presence. He wanted her to come to him willingly with the passion he sensed burning barely beneath her surface.

Or was he projecting what he felt on the woman? He struggled to contain his passion whenever she was around.

It had taken over a year to rebuild his confidence and any trust in his ability to attract a woman. He chalked that up to the fallout of his fiancée leaving him for the maid of honor.

Yeah, women readily responded to his appearance, but he didn't trust any of them or his own judgment. He'd failed colossally once. He'd be damned if it happened again.

Rafael hadn't spent much time with any one woman since, as disinclined as he was to let one get close.

There were plenty who were still willing when he

was upfront that he didn't come with strings and that he had no intention of committing to a relationship.

If a woman didn't want his attentions—which was never the case—he would simply move on.

Then why couldn't he let go of this one?

When he'd kissed her the night before, she'd been surprised, but she'd leaned into him as if she'd wanted more. When he'd tempted her with the near-kiss that morning, he could swear she'd swayed toward him. Though he hadn't actually kissed her, her lips had puckered ever so slightly when his thumb had brushed across them.

Still, she'd shown him the door and told him she didn't need him anymore.

Would that make him a stalker if he didn't take the hint? Should he back down and leave her alone?

Gisele held out a padded envelope to YaYa. "I actually came over to give you this package. The delivery driver dropped it one building short." Gisele gave YaYa a tight smile, threw a quick glance his way without actually meeting his eyes and turned toward her shop. "I'd better get back to work. Congrats on the added clients."

Without saying goodbye, so long or you're an ass to Rafael, Gisele walked away.

If he was reading her right, she'd just wordlessly told him to fuck off.

Challenge accepted.

He didn't delve into his need to bring her around

to him. Maybe it was pride that wouldn't let him give up.

Rafael shook his head. No. It was her dark hair, darker eyes, light brown skin and mostly her feisty attitude that kept him in the game.

She intrigued him.

"If you want her, you have to make an effort," YaYa's voice broke through his intense focus on Gisele's disappearing figure.

He frowned and dragged his attention back to the woman standing at his side. "Excuse me?"

"If you want her, you have to earn her trust and show her that you're not like most men."

"What are most men like to her?" he asked, intensely eager to know the answer.

"To Gisele, most men stay in a relationship until it no longer benefits them, or they grow bored."

"Is she divorced?" Rafael asked.

"No, thank goodness. She had the good sense to end a toxic relationship after her boyfriend threw her under the bus for a promotion when they worked at the same company in New York City."

Rafael couldn't picture her in a business suit. Though she'd be sexy as hell in one. "Gisele worked in New York City?"

YaYa nodded. "On Wall Street. She never fit in. Our girl has morals. She left here, ready to take on the world. She came back with huge trust issues when it comes to men. She hasn't been on a date since she bought the shop. That was three years ago."

"Her boyfriend threw her under the bus?" Rafael shook his head. "How?"

"I don't know the whole story. Just that she refused to do something unethical. Her boyfriend stepped up to the plate. Not only did he perform the unethical deed, but he also claimed Gisele was incompetent and not a team player. He told their boss that he was willing to do whatever it took, no questions asked."

That would explain a lot about why Gisele was so standoffish with him. She didn't have any reason to trust him. Or any man. Why should she? The one she'd thought cared about her had shown his true colors, tainting all men with his betrayal.

The fact that they both had trust issues wasn't lost on Rafael. He should be a decent human and walk away from the petite yet sultry gift shop owner. She didn't want or need someone like him to make her life any more miserable than that NYC asshat had already managed.

She had her little shop. She seemed happy enough without a man in her life. Why screw it up?

However, there was the matter of the burglar.

Rafael could stick around only to make sure she was safe.

He should ignore the fact that she ticked every box on his list of what he wanted in a woman.

His failed attempt at marriage and his vow to avoid the institution at all costs made him a poor match for Gisele.

She deserved a really nice guy who would worship the ground she walked on and do everything in his power to love, honor and protect her, even if it meant sacrificing his life for hers.

"You really like her, don't you?" YaYa asked.

He'd been so deep in his thoughts he'd forgotten where he was and who was watching him. He forced a shrug. "I worry that she isn't taking the burglary seriously enough."

"She needs a security system with surveillance cameras and alarms." YaYa studied him. "Think you can use all that masculine charm and charisma to talk her into such a thing?"

His lips twisted. "I'm not sure my so-called charm works with her."

YaYa laughed. "Honey, she practically ran back to her shop."

"My point exactly," he said.

YaYa faced him, her brow dipping low over her forehead. "She ran because she's scared."

"Of me?"

"Not of you," YaYa said. "Of herself."

He shook his head. "I don't understand."

"She's afraid to let down her guard. Afraid of giving her trust to someone who could potentially hurt her."

"I wouldn't hurt her."

YaYa cocked an eyebrow. "Wouldn't you?"

"I'd never lie to her," Rafael said. "I'd tell her the truth and let her make up her own mind."

"Even if the truth would be just as hurtful as a lie?" YaYa asked quietly.

He stared into the Mamba Wamba Gift Shop window, searching for Gisele.

He'd always assumed that if he told the women he saw the truth about not wanting strings or commitment, it would be less painful when it came time to leave.

Was it?

When had he gone back to the women he'd dated and left behind to ask if his abrupt departure had caused them pain?

Never.

Wow. That made him as big an asshat as the man who'd thrown Gisele under the bus.

"I don't want to hurt her," Rafael said. "But I do want to make sure she's safe."

"Then make her safe." She laid her hand on his arm. "But leave her heart to someone who won't break it." She lifted her chin toward the second-story windows. "And don't be a peeping Tom."

Rafael held up a hand. "For security reasons only."

YaYa snorted. "Right." The older woman turned away.

"YaYa," Rafael called out.

She looked over her shoulder. "Yes?"

"You're a good friend to Gisele."

"She'd give me the shirt off her back," YaYa said. "Don't hurt her."

Rafael nodded. "Yes, ma'am."

Her eyes narrowed. "And don't call me ma'am. I'm not that much older than you." Her face softened. "But I do wish I was at least fifteen years younger when I'm with you. I like to think I would've stood a chance." She sighed.

"You're a beautiful woman, YaYa." He tapped a fist to his chest. "Where it counts most."

She laughed. "Oh, please. That's like having a good personality."

"When you have a good heart, a good personality and friends," he said, "you have enough. You *are* enough."

"Your words are as pretty as your face, Rafael Romero. Be sure your actions match." With that last bit of advice, she entered her studio.

The women who'd been lined up in the alley followed.

Valentin approached, clapped a hand on Rafael's back and grinned. "That was the last box. Remy and Gerard had to go. They said they'd see you later and to call if you need any more help." He tipped his head toward the yoga studio. "What did your landlord have to say?"

"To make myself at home," Rafael said, "but don't leave any damage."

"Words to live by, my friend," Valentin said. "Words to live by."

Rafael shot one more glance toward the Mamba Wamba Gift Shop before he turned toward his truck. "Are we still on for the noon meeting at the boat factory?"

Valentin nodded, falling into step beside Rafael. "Remy got word from Hank Patterson. One of Sadie's friends requested a protector detail to provide security while she shoots a music video in New Orleans." He grinned. "I wouldn't mind spending some time in the Big Easy."

"It's not like you'll get to enjoy the food and nightlife. You'll be on the job."

"I know, but there's always something interesting to see or good music to hear." Valentin tipped his head toward the bayou. "All I hear around here are frogs, cicadas and Cajun drunks calling each other names."

"What about the Zydeco festival?" Rafael asked.

Valentin shrugged. "The festival has been going for three days. Zydeco was fun, for a change, the first night. I'm ready to go back and relax with classic bands like Led Zeppelin, AC/DC and Disturbed."

Rafael's lips twisted. "How are you hooked on music from the last century?"

Valentin frowned. "It's timeless. My father played

hard rock music whenever he was home. He swore it stimulated the mind. I think it was more a case of stimulating his sex drive."

Rafael held up a hand. "You can stop right there. I don't need to know the details about your parents' sex life."

"I was conceived to some of Led Zeppelin's greatest hits," Valentin admitted with his hand resting on his chest as if paying tribute to the greats.

Rafael pressed his hands over his ears. "I told you. I don't need to relive the sexual act that resulted in your birth and subsequent mark on all of mankind."

Valentin grinned. "Suit yourself."

"Besides, it's not hard rock you'll get in New Orleans," Rafael pointed out. "There's more jazz there than anything else."

Valentin shrugged. "I could get into some Louis Armstrong and Ella Fitzgerald-style music." He grinned. "It's New Orleans. What's not to love?"

Rafael grinned. "True." Yet he hoped Remy wasn't considering sending him there for the security detail. He didn't want to leave Bayou Mambaloa until they knew a little more about the break-in at the Mamba Wamba Gift Shop.

Truth was, he didn't want to leave Gisele unprotected.

She had her assistant during the day, but she was alone at night with no one to have her back.

Now that he had the apartment across from hers,

he was at least within yelling distance and could be there in seconds.

When Rafael reached his truck, he slipped in behind the steering wheel, his gaze on the little gift shop.

Valentin climbed into the passenger seat. "You're going to opt out of the New Orleans gig, aren't you?"

Rafael shot a frown toward Valentin. "Why do you think that?"

"Dude, it's pretty obvious that you're stuck on the gift shop owner. Though I'm not convinced she's that into you." He held up a hand. "Don't worry. I won't interfere. I think she's hot, but I get it. You have first dibs."

"You can't have dibs on women," Rafael said. "They tend to make up their own minds."

"Well, I'll give Ms. Gautier a week to decide before I turn my brand of charm on her. After that, you won't have a snowball's chance in hell to win her back."

Rafael snorted. "Am I supposed to thank you for the courtesy?"

"You could. Or you could turn up the Romeo appeal and see where it gets you." He glanced at his watch. "One week, man. That's all the courtesy I'll give you. Better get cracking."

Rafael frowned. "And what are your intentions toward Gisele?"

Valentin blinked. "Asks the man who goes

through women like a revolving door. Why do you care? Maybe I just want a date or two. There aren't a whole lot of choices in Bayou Mambaloa, and she's pretty. If things work out, I might consider a longer commitment. I'm not allergic to the idea, like you. Now that I'm not in the military, I might want to settle down, get married and have a family."

"Wait a minute." Rafael frowned at Valentin. "I thought you said you didn't like kids, which was why you left the Navy."

Valentin nodded. "I might have said that. I didn't want to be stuck babysitting a bunch of kids going through BUD/S training. I don't have the patience."

"Why didn't you stay on a team?" Rafael asked.

"An injury slowed me down. They only gave me one choice."

"BUD/S." Rafael nodded.

"I took option two and left the Navy. I didn't want to be tied down."

"Why the big turnaround?" Rafael started the truck engine. "Having a family means a wife and kids. That's not just tying down, that's anchoring."

"It might not be so bad," Valentin stared at the gift shop, "with the right woman."

Rafael's hand rested on the shift, his gaze pinned on Valentin. "Since I've known you, you've been standoffish with women. Why are you all of a sudden interested in Gisele Gautier? Are you just trying to piss me off?"

Valentin's lips quirked slightly, though his attention remained on the gift shop. "Is it working?"

Rafael slammed the shift into drive, his foot on the brake. "It sure as hell is. What's your end game?"

"Does it matter? It's not like you plan on marrying the girl. You've told me on several occasions you'll never stand at an altar again. I just hate to see you toying with this woman and then leaving her dangling for too long. She deserves better."

It was a good thing his fist was curled around the steering wheel. At that moment, he wanted to plant it in his friend's face. Rafael breathed in and out before continuing the conversation. "Are you saying I'm not good enough for her?"

Valentin sighed. "No. I'm not saying that you're not good enough for her. You're a great guy with the team. You'd take a bullet for any one of us, and we'd do the same for you. But when it comes to women... Not all women are your ex-fiancée. You can't paint them with the same brush. Gisele is a nice lady with a lot of gumption. I'd hate to see her hurt."

"By me," Rafael added. Some of his anger dissipated at the truth in his friend's words.

Valentin nodded. "By you. You might not be ready to let go of the past, and that will keep you from finding happiness in your future."

Rafael shook his head. "When did you decide to become my therapist?"

"I didn't," Valentin said, refusing to meet Rafael's gaze. "I drew the short straw."

"What short straw?" Rafael demanded.

Valentin didn't respond.

His eyes narrowing, Rafael studied his teammate. "Have you and the rest of the guys been discussing me behind my back?"

A flood of ruddy red stained Valentin's cheeks. "I told them I didn't think this would go over well," he muttered.

What the ever-loving fuck? Rafael was floored. "I can't believe you've all been talking about me."

"Yeah, get pissed, but consider this an intervention. We're your friends, and we're concerned that you're on a self-destructive track."

"Why feel the need to intervene now?" he demanded.

Valentin glanced away. "We've always been concerned. It's just that some of the guys are hearing it from their women that they're worried you'll break Gisele's heart."

The anger was back ten-fold. "You can tell the guys to kiss my ass. Gisele's capable of making her own decisions. I've never lied to a woman to get her into my bed. I won't start now."

"Just because she goes into a relationship with you with her eyes wide open, doesn't mean she won't lose her heart. You're pretty potent shit to females, like catnip to felines." Valentin shrugged again. "Or so

I've heard. Anyway, if you're going with your same modus operandi of love 'em and leave 'em, you're going to make the womenfolk mad. In turn, they'll make their men mad at you."

Rafael wanted to tell Valentin and his entire team to go fuck themselves.

But he'd been heading down that same path of reasoning. Not so much about everyone in Bayou Mambaloa being mad at him, but that he'd hurt Gisele. He really didn't want to hurt her.

His best course of action would be to step away from the female and let her get on with her life sans one former Navy SEAL.

One thing bothered him more than he cared to admit. "What you said about making your move on Gisele...were you serious? Are you interested in her for more than just a date of two? Or was that your way of getting my goat or making me step aside and leave her alone?"

Valentin's lips curled upward. "She's really pretty. I like that she's independent, self-sufficient and fully capable of standing on her own. Any guy would be lucky to have her, including me."

"You're not answering my question," Rafael said through gritted teeth.

"I like her. But I'm not in the market for a long-term relationship. And I'm not willing to take the risk of stirring the hornet's nest of our team and their women." He glanced over the console at Rafael.

"So, no. I'm not really interested in going after Gisele. Like her girlfriends say, she deserves someone who's all in, head over heels in love with her and who would do anything to earn her respect and love in return."

Rafael stared at his friend and teammate for a long moment. Valentin, one of the most stoic of their team, a man who kept to himself and rarely spoke out about anyone, had just spoken more words in the past half hour than Rafael had heard him speak in a week. It had to have been a challenge for him.

Rafael lifted his foot off the brake and pulled onto Main Street, heading for the other end of town and the old boat factory they'd converted into the Bayou Brotherhood Protectors regional office. "You really did get the short straw, didn't you?"

"Yeah," Valentin said. "And it sucked balls." He was silent for a minute and then asked, "You good?"

Rafael snorted. "What do you think?"

Valentin's lips twisted. "You're mad as hell."

"I can't say that I like my so-called friends interfering in my personal life," Rafael said, "but, yeah, I'm good. I heard what you said, and I'll keep it in mind."

Another minute passed.

"Are you going to stop seeing Gisele?" Valentin asked.

"I said I'm good," Rafael said through gritted teeth. "Don't test me."

He wanted to drop Valentin off at the boat factory

for their team meeting and skip it himself, but he wouldn't let his *friends* have the satisfaction of knowing Valentin's short-straw speech had hit home.

Because it had, echoing what he'd already begun to realize.

Gisele was special. Her friends recognized it and were looking out for her.

He pasted a smile on his face and strode into the warm room at the boat factory, enjoying the tension fully visible on Valentin's face and the exchange of glances between him and the other members of the team. He wouldn't rise to the intervention they'd launched, and he had no intention of informing them of his plans when it came to Gisele.

Mostly because he didn't know what they were—other than to make sure she was safe. Beyond that...

Hell.

He had no idea.

The logical side of his brain told him to cut his losses and leave her alone. That way, she wouldn't be subjected to his bad habits and left with a broken heart when he pulled his duck-and-run routine.

The devil on his shoulder screamed louder than logic.

You know you want her.

She wants you, too.

Don't let the goodie-two-shoes talk you out of holding her in your arms and making love to her through the night.

His groin tightened.

He sat still, willing his libido to calm the fuck down as he listened to Hank Patterson brief them on the New Orleans security project.

Hank, the founder of Brotherhood Protectors, was a giant head on the display screen, projecting his image from his home in Montana. "The assignment will last a week, maybe more, if the filming takes longer.

"We'll need five men in New Orleans tomorrow to augment the singer's own security team."

Remy turned to the men seated around the table. "I'm going, along with Gerard, Lucas and Valentin." Remy's eyes narrowed as he glanced around the room. "Beau starts a bodyguard job tomorrow with Senator Anderson and his daughter. Jacques and Xavier are already out on different assignments, which leaves Landry and Rafael."

Without pausing to think, Rafael said, "As much as I'd like a fun-filled paid trip to New Orleans, I'd like to remain in Bayou Mambaloa."

Hank met Rafael's gaze through the video conference call. "Did they find the intruder who broke into Ms. Gautier's shop?"

Rafael shook his head. "No, sir."

"Has there been another attack?" Hank asked.

"No, sir," Rafael repeated. "But I have a gut feeling she's not out of danger yet. She lives alone in the apartment over the shop with no backup. I just moved into the apartment across the alley from her. I'd like to hang around for a couple of days to make sure she doesn't have a repeat of what happened last night."

"Any clue as to what the burglar was after?" Hank asked.

"No, sir," Remy responded. "The sheriff's department is conducting the investigation, but they don't have much to go on. He wore gloves, so no fingerprints. A ski mask hid his facial features. He didn't take anything, but he trashed a shelf and tipped over a bird cage."

"Anyone injured on the grounds?" Hank asked. "Ms. Gautier?"

"The intruder slammed into Ms. Gautier on his way out the back door. She was shaken but okay. I can monitor her situation on my own time," Rafael offered, "since she hasn't asked us to step in and provide her with a bodyguard."

"That's not necessary. We don't only cater to people who can pay," Hank said. "My wife and I want people to have access to our services no matter their financial status. When they need help, we want them to know they can count on us, no matter their ability to pay."

Rafael nodded. "Then I'll keep an eye on her and her shop for a few days to ensure the attack was a crime of opportunity that won't happen again."

"Makes sense," Hank said. "Does she have a security system?"

"No, sir."

"Encourage her to get one. Surveillance videos would've been handy for the investigators."

"I'll work on her," Rafael said. "I'll see what we can rig in the meantime."

Hank looked around at the room full of men. "Then Landry will be your fifth man going to New Orleans?"

Remy shot a glance toward Valentin and then to Rafael. "Sounds like it."

"Good. Then I'll leave you to the arrangements. Thank you all for being members of the Brotherhood Protectors," Hank said. "Out here."

His image blipped off the screen, leaving it glowing a bright blue.

Remy looked around the room. "Anyone have any questions?"

Landry turned to Rafael. "I could keep an eye on Ms. Gautier if you'd rather participate in the New Orleans project."

Rafael's jaw hardened. It took a full second for him to force a smile. "As much as I like visiting New Orleans, I need to see the Gautier assignment through."

Landry nodded. "Fair enough."

"Those heading to New Orleans tomorrow can stay," Remy said. "The rest of you are dismissed."

Rafael stood and started to leave without saying anything...but he couldn't.

He faced the entire team and said, "It's good to know you all have Ms. Gautier's best interests at heart. Let me set your minds at ease. So. Do. I."

He didn't wait for a response.

Rafael spun on his heels and left the boat factory, climbed into his truck and drove back to Main Street and the apartment he'd just moved into. He needed the time to cool down, unwind and unpack.

Thankfully, he had a clear view of the Mamba Wamba from his bedroom window. He'd stop in later that afternoon to check on his self-proclaimed client.

On a strictly professional basis.

Valentin would be happy to know.

Message received...loud and clear.

CHAPTER 7

WITH THE ZYDECO Festival still in full swing, business was steady. Tourists filtered through the shop, purchasing voodoo dolls, gris-gris amulets, Gisele's Motion Lotion, LP#9 and other remedies advertised as infused with voodoo magic.

She'd sent Lena out to get lunch for them from the diner and hadn't had time to eat her chicken Caesar salad. Every time there was a lull in the flow of customers, she'd dash back to her salad. Before she could take a bite, the door would open, and more people would enter.

Lena could handle questions about different products or voodoo customs as well as Gisele could, but someone had to run the register while the other fielded those questions.

Thirty minutes before she was due to close the shop, a heavyset teenage girl stormed through the door, blond hair flying, her face red and angry. She slammed a bottle on the counter in front of Gisele and demanded, "I want my money back."

Gisele calmly lifted the bottle and noted the label —LP #9. "I don't normally offer refunds for my lotions and potions. Could I have a name, please?" she asked in her calmest tone.

"My name is Lana Dafani, and I want my money back."

"What seems to be the problem, Miss Dafani?" Gisele asked.

"This potion didn't work," Lana said, her voice rising. "In fact, it had the opposite effect of what I expected."

Gisele studied the girl's face. Her lips looked like any normal teenager's lips. Not having seen her before applying the potion, she couldn't tell if it had worked. "Did you follow the instructions that came with it?"

"What instructions? There were no instructions."

Gisele shook her head. "Every bottle of LP#9 is sold with instructions printed on the label affixed to the back of the bottle, and either my assistant or I go over those instructions before a bottle leaves the shop." She held up the bottle and pointed to the back label.

The girl squinted at the label. "Oh, those. Yes. I did what it said. It didn't work, I tell you."

"I also record the names of those who purchase

it." Gisele booted her computer and brought up the database of customers and products purchased by each. "I know I didn't speak with you." Gisele turned to Lena. "Did you sell Miss Dafani this bottle of LP#9?"

Lena shook her head. "I did not. I'd remember her if I did."

Gisele searched for the teen's name in her database. "I'm sorry, your name isn't coming up."

"I didn't buy it," the girl said. "My mother purchased it. I used it, and I want our money back. It didn't work. It's dangerous and shouldn't be sold. I should sue you for everything you own for what it did."

Gisele shook her head. "I'm sorry, but you'll have to be more specific. Can you explain to me what it allegedly did?"

"Tell you?" She snorted. "I'll show you." She stormed out of the shop.

Lena leaned over Gisele's shoulder. "We've never had a problem with the LP#9 lip plumper."

Gisele checked her database for any other Dafani. "I have a Beatrice Dafani in the system. She's a forty-two-year-old woman who lives in a small town to the west of Bayou Mambaloa. She purchased the bottle on the first day of the Zydeco Festival."

"We were both here," Lena said.

"The sale was recorded, so one of us spoke to her mother about how to test it on a small patch of skin to make sure she doesn't have an allergic reaction to the ingredients in the formula."

The blond teen burst through the door again, dragging a young man behind her.

He wore a hoodie pulled up over his head and walked with his head down, his face hidden in shadows.

Lana came to a halt in front of the counter and swung the young man around to stand beside her. "This is what your poison did." She yanked the hoodie down and pointed to the teenage boy's face.

The boy's cheeks flushed a mottled red as he stood before them. He looked like any teenage boy with a smattering of whiskers not yet thick enough to form a beard. It was his lips that had Gisele concerned. They were swollen to over three times puffier than normal.

"Oh, sweetie." Gisele came around the counter. "What's your name?"

"Dewek," he said, his words garbled by the size of his lips.

Gisele spoke to the young man in a calm and soothing voice. "How much of the potion did you use?

"I didn't use it," he said. "Not intentionawy." He glared at Lana. "She put it on my wip bawm."

"Your lip balm?" Gisele asked.

He nodded. "I had chapped wips."

Gisele frowned at Lana. "When we sell this, we

very specifically tell the purchaser not to use it on chapped lips." She turned a gentle smile on Derek. "How many times did you apply the lip plumper?"

"Lip plumper?" Lana said, her gaze going from Gisele to Lena and back to Gisele. "What lip plumper?"

Gisele's brow dipped low. "LP#9 is lip plumper. You knew that, right?" She pointed to the back label again. "Lip Plumper #9. Right above the instructions."

Lana leaned closer, her eyes widening. "No way. That wasn't there. I swear it wasn't."

Lena pulled another bottle out from beneath the counter and showed her the back label. "It's on every bottle of LP#9 that goes out of the shop."

Lana shook her head.

Gisele turned her attention back to Derek. "How many times did you apply the balm?"

He shrugged. "I don't know. Thwee or fo times...evewy houwa unti my wips swelled wike dis." He pointed to his swollen mouth and then glared at Lana. "Why would you spike my wip bawm with wip pwumpa?"

All the anger leached out of Lana's face, leaving it pale and drawn. "I thought it was a love potion," she whispered with a stricken expression.

"Wuv potion?" Derek's frown deepened. "What da fuck, Wana?"

Lana shrank back. "I thought that if you loved me, you'd finally ask me out. We've been friends for so long. I didn't want to be just friends anymore. I wanted you to love me as more than a friend. I wanted you to be my first date. My first kiss."

Derek's frown softened. "You did?" He reached for her hand.

Lana took it. "I love you."

"I wuv you, too."

Lana's eyes widened. "You do?"

He nodded.

"It wasn't the love potion?" she asked and then shook her head. "No, wait, it wasn't a love potion." Her face brightened into a watery smile. "It was lip plumper." She lifted his hand to her cheek. "You really love me?"

Derek nodded. "I ahways have."

Lana turned to Gisele. "Thank you. This place is truly magical. He loves me."

Lena frowned. "It wasn't a love po—"

Gisele elbowed her assistant gently in the side. "My potions bring out the truth that's already inside," Gisele said.

"Yes, yes, of course." Lana leaned into the teenager and stared up into his eyes. A frown sent her eyebrows back down, forming a V over the bridge of her nose. "Do you have a potion to counteract the lip plumper?"

Gisele nodded. "Of course I do. Wait here. I'll be right back."

Lena frowned as Gisele walked past her. "We have a counter agent?" she whispered.

"We do," Gisele assured her. She walked into the small bathroom at the rear of the shop and dug in the cabinet until she found what she was looking for. She poured a medicine cup full of the special elixir that would set Derek on a course to full recovery and carried it out to the afflicted teen. "This is my grand-mère's go-to tonic for overdoses of LP#9. Drink up. It might take a few hours for the magic to work, but by morning, you should be just fine."

Derek managed to pour the fluid past his swollen lips and swallowed. He handed the little cup to Gisele and gave her a distorted smile. "Thank you."

"Thank you." Lana hugged Gisele, whispering in her ear, "If not for you, I might never have known Derek loved me. You really are magical."

Gisele smiled and waved a hand toward the contents of her little shop, giving it a touch of drama. "I only use Voodoo to help people," she said.

"Well, you helped us." Lana smiled, tucked her hand into the crook of Derek's elbow and left the shop a lot happier than when she'd blown through the door minutes before.

Gisele's gaze followed the young couple until movement near Johnny's cage caught her attention.

Rafael stepped out into the open, a smile spreading across his face.

"How long have you been standing there?" Gisele asked.

"Long enough to bond with your feathered friend." He tipped his head toward the entrance. "I came in behind the lovebirds."

"So, you saw all that?"

He nodded. "I did. You might want to consider renaming LP#9."

Gisele sighed. "I thought it was a fun play on Love Potion #9, and I've been very careful to tell customers it's not a love potion but a lip plumper." She shook her head. "But you're right; it's time to rethink the name."

Lena walked past Gisele, slinging her backpack over her shoulder. "I hope you and your man don't need me to stay late. I have a date for the concert tonight at the festival. Want me to turn the sign over?"

"Please," Gisele called out to her assistant as the younger woman reached the entrance.

Lena flipped the sign from OPEN to CLOSED. She paused in the doorway. "You'll have to show me where to find the elixir to counter LP#9 in case I need it for another overdose."

"Tomorrow," Gisele called out with a grin.

Lena left the shop with a wave.

Gisele followed her to the door and twisted the deadbolt. Then she turned and leaned against the door, aware that she'd just locked herself in with

Rafael. A shiver of excitement almost reenergized her tired body. "What a day."

"I bet you're tired," he said. "You've had a constant flow of customers all day."

She nodded. "Nothing like a little drama to cap it off." Gisele pushed away from the door and walked back to the counter where Lana's bottle of LP#9 sat next to the empty medicine cup. "Someday, I'll look back on that little episode and laugh." She smiled. "I'm just too tired right now. Poor Derek."

"You have antidotes for all your potions?" Rafael asked.

"No," she said and scooped up the medicine cup and lip plumper bottle. "But I have a bottle of liquid antihistamine in my first aid kit for allergic reactions to peanuts, wasp stings, mosquito bites," she snorted and held up the hand with the bottle in it, "and now LP#9."

Rafael chuckled, the sound warm and intoxicating.

Gisele could get drunk on his laughter. Or was she just weak from hunger? "Can I help you with something?"

"No. But I might be able to help you." He held up a bag. "I brought you a present."

She swayed toward the bag, a little lightheaded. "If it's food, I'll love you forever."

His lips twisted. "Sorry. It's not food. However, I whipped up a pot of taco soup in my apartment. Play your cards right, and I'll share with you…after I install your present."

Her mouth watered at the prospect of taco soup. "You certainly know a woman's love language."

He grinned. "I thought food was a *man's* love language."

"I've always been different. Ask anybody."

"I like different," he said, his eyes warm and friendly.

Her guard was way down. If she wasn't careful, she'd do something stupid, like ask him to kiss her again.

Focus, woman.

She nodded toward the bag. "What can I help you install so we can make it quick and get to that taco soup?"

He dug into the bag and pulled out several devices. "These are only a temporary solution until you can install that security and surveillance system I know you called about today."

"Right. I had nothing else to do today." She shook her head. "The festival will be winding down after tomorrow. I won't be as swamped. Besides, I couldn't have called today anyway. I'm sure none of the installers answer their phones on the weekend."

"Good point."

She studied the devices he laid out on the counter. "What do we have here?"

"Alarms," he said. "I can install one on every door

and window in a few minutes. If someone tries to get in, the alarm will screech loud enough to wake the dead."

She cocked an eyebrow. "You tested it in a cemetery? How many bodies did you raise?"

He chucked his finger beneath her chin. "Don't get cheeky, little girl."

Cheeky bastard, Johnny squawked.

Rafael chuckled again, the sound seeping into her skin like warm syrup.

God, she was too tired to fight the desire rising inside.

Get me a beer, woman, Johnny called out, giving Gisele the needed wake-up call to move away from the man before she lost herself in his chuckle and promises of taco soup.

"I'm just going to feed Johnny. Yell if you need me." She tore herself away from the man and hurried to fill Johnny's feed dish with seed. "I'll be back in a minute," she called out.

Gisele left through the back door and trudged up the stairs to her apartment.

As she slipped her key into the lock, footsteps pounded up behind her. Out of the corner of her eye, she could see Rafael hurrying up to her.

Rather than argue, she unlocked the door and stepped back, waving a hand for him to go inside before her.

"Good girl," he said, bent and brushed her lips

with his, "you know the drill." A frown dented his brow. "Sorry. I shouldn't have done that."

He disappeared inside before she could ask him why he shouldn't have done that when she wanted him to do *that* again.

Gisele raised her fingers to her lips. They still tingled from that rare brush with perfection. She really wanted him to do that again.

She practically fell through the door, intent on cornering him and insisting he kiss her again.

Rafael emerged from her bedroom. "All clear."

Though she stood directly in front of him, he sidestepped her and headed for the exit, leaving before she could speak.

"What the fuck?" she murmured.

Talk about mixed messages. He showed up with presents, offered her food, kissed her and then apologized and ran out before she could ask him to do it again.

"Who was that man?" she asked the air.

Gisele shook her head and looked around her apartment, trying to remember why she'd come up there in the first place.

Oh, yeah.

Johnny wanted a beer.

She grabbed a mango from the counter, cut it in half, fished some lettuce from the refrigerator and headed back down the stairs a little slower this time. She wasn't sure how she should act around Dr.

Jekyll...or was he Mr. Hyde?

She decided to pretend like nothing weird had happened rather than call him out on it and look like the weird one.

Rafael was at the back door, screwing one of the devices into the doorframe with a battery-operated drill.

She paused, wondering whether she should wait until he was done or...

A smile pulled at the corners of her lips. Instead of waiting for him to finish, she squeezed in behind him, pressing her breasts against his back in order to make it through the sliver of space between him and the doorframe.

He stiffened, his hand freezing, the drill bit spinning in the air.

That got his attention.

Once through, she walked away, crossing one foot in front of the other like a model on a runway.

The drill quit whirring.

Gisele glanced over her shoulder to gauge Rafael's reaction to her version of vamping.

His gaze was on her.

In time to see her trip over her own feet and land in a graceless heap. The mango half flew from her hand, rolling to a stop beneath Johnny's cage.

You break it, you buy it, asshole, the bird said.

A burst of laughter rang out behind her as Rafael reached her. "Sorry. Sometimes, I forget Johnny's a bird. He has a comedian's timing." He dropped to his haunches. "Are you hurt?"

Her lips twisted. "Yes."

"Here?" Rafael reached out and ran his hands over her legs.

Her heart skipped several beats, then pounded against her ribs. "No," she breathed.

"Here?" His fingers skimmed up her arms, tickling the soft undersides.

She giggled and squirmed. "No."

"Then where?" he demanded, his hands traveling down her sides, tickling her relentlessly.

Gisele squealed and tried to wiggle her way free. "Stop..." she gasped. "Not fair..."

Immediately, his hands stilled.

Her breath grew ragged as she stared up into eyes almost as black as his hair. He was leaning over her, his face so close she could feel his warm breath against her skin.

"Then tell me where it hurts so I can kiss it better," he said,

His voice, so deep and husky, sent shivers of desire coursing through her veins.

She raised a finger and pointed to her cheek.

Rafael pressed his lips to the spot. "Here?"

She nodded and pointed to her other cheek.

He kissed that point. "Better?"

Again, she nodded. Then she touched her finger

to her lips. Her breath lodged in her chest as silent seconds passed and he didn't move.

He didn't want to kiss her. He really wasn't that into her. He didn't find her attractive. She was making a complete fool of herself.

Her heart squeezed so hard inside it hurt.

Then, like a light switch being flipped on, Rafael let out a groan. "Oh, hell," he muttered. "Who am I kidding?" His mouth crashed down on hers, wiping away all her self-doubt and filling her with acceptance, confidence and...hot, raging desire.

She wrapped her arms around his neck and held him to her, deepening the kiss he'd started.

Her leg wrapped around his calf and slid up the back of his knee to his thigh, bringing him closer still.

It wasn't close enough. Her fingers searched for and found the button on his jeans and flipped it free.

His hand tugged her blouse from her skirt and slid beneath to cup her breast.

As her fingers wrapped around the tab of his zipper, a loud, raucous squawk broke through her haze of desire.

Cheeky bastard, Johnny said.

"Ignore him," Gisele whispered.

Bring me a beer, woman, Johnny persisted.

Gisele and Rafael remain motionless, her hand frozen on his zipper tab, his hand cupping her breast.

A moment of silence passed. Then another.

Gisele released the breath she'd been holding. "See? If we ignore him, he'll—"

A knock sounded on the door to the front entrance.

"Can't they read the sign?" she whispered. "We're closed. Ignore it."

The knocking stopped.

Rafael's hand squeezed her breast gently.

Gisele slid the zipper down a couple of teeth.

"Gisele?" a female voice called through the back door.

Gisele lifted her head enough to see a woman stepping over something at the threshold.

Rafael grabbed her and rolled her to the side and out of view of the woman heading their way. He leaped to his feet, yanked her up onto hers and helped her tuck her shirt into the waistband of her skirt.

They turned to face the woman rounding the corner of the hallway, dressed in a sheriff deputy's maternity uniform.

CHAPTER 8

GISELE PASTED a smile on her face, hoping she didn't look like she felt—flushed, tousled and sexually aroused.

"Oh, there you are," Shelby Taylor exclaimed. "I was getting worried. You didn't answer my knock on the front door. When I found the back door wide open, I thought you might be in trouble." Her gaze swept over Rafael, and her eyes narrowed. "Are you in trouble?"

Gisele forced a laugh that sounded more like a strangled squeak and smoothed her hair back from her face. "Not at all. I tripped over my own feet a moment ago. Rafael was just helping me."

"Helping you, was he?" Shelby muttered something beneath her breath that sounded like, "Or helping himself to you?"

"Yes, he was," Gisele smiled brightly. "He's

installing temporary alarms on all the doors and windows until I can have a security system installed."

Shelby's eyes remained narrow as she studied Rafael. Then she turned to Gisele. "I came by to see if you would join me at the Crawdad Hole for dinner. Remy is still at the office, gearing up for a gig in the city. Junior and I could use the company." The deputy patted her barely showing pregnant belly.

Gisele opened her mouth to decline the invitation. Before she could, Rafael spoke up.

"You should go with your friend," Rafael said. "No need for you to stick around. I'll finish here and lock up when I'm done. Just leave me a key to the front door."

"But—" she started to remind him that he'd offered her taco soup. She *wanted* taco soup.

"No buts," he said. "I insist. You've had a busy day; you need a chance to unwind." He gave her a tight smile. "Girl time."

"That's right. Girl time. Besides, I worked through lunch, and I'm starving." Shelby motioned toward the counter. "Grab your purse. Let's go."

After Gisele grudgingly gave Rafael the spare front door key and grabbed her purse, Shelby hustled Gisele through the shop and out the back door. As Shelby passed Rafael, her gaze dropped to his...package. "Your barn door is open. You might want to zip it."

Rafael's hand rose automatically to the offending zipper.

Heat burned all the way up Gisele's neck into her cheeks. She shot an apologetic glance over her shoulder at Rafael.

Shelby hooked her arm and half-dragged her around to the front of the shop and into her SUV.

As she slid behind the wheel, Shelby said, "I have to make a quick stop at my house to change. It won't take me two shakes and we can be at the Crawdad Hole in no time."

Gisele sat silently as Shelby drove to her place and parked. She remained in her seat as Shelby got out.

Her friend bent and peered across the cab. "Don't you want to come in?"

Gisele gave her a weak smile. "If you're not going to be long and don't need help, I'll just wait here."

Shelby shrugged. "I won't even be five minutes. I'm just going to get out of my uniform and into something more comfortable."

"I'll be here," Gisele said.

Shelby shut the door and hurried into her cottage.

Gisele sat in the passenger seat, going over the last few minutes she'd spent with Rafael. They'd been hot and heavy, well on their way to getting naked on the floor of the shop in broad daylight! He'd been just as turned on by her as she'd been by him.

Then he'd gone cold and had practically pushed her out the door with Shelby.

And why had Shelby given him the stink-eye? She'd never seen her friend act so unfriendly toward one of her husband's teammates.

Gisele hadn't wanted to go with Shelby and had half a mind to fake a headache and ask her to take her back to the shop. At least then she could corner Rafael and get to the bottom of why he kept going from hot to cold, back to hot and then cold again.

He was giving her whiplash.

True to her word, Shelby was back in less than five minutes. She'd changed from her uniform into jeans, a tank top and a white button-down shirt that hung loosely around her hips. At five months along, she barely looked pregnant. She'd pulled the elastic band out of her long blond hair and brushed it smooth to hang down around her shoulders, making her appear more feminine. She was still the kickass deputy but with softer edges.

They'd been friends growing up, but they'd been so busy with their respective careers they hadn't spent much time together lately. And it was even harder to get together since Remy had come home to Bayou Mambaloa.

Shelby grinned as she climbed into the SUV. "It's been too long since we went out together," she said, echoing Gisele's thoughts. "I'm glad Remy's occupied tonight. We needed this time to catch up. Once the baby's born, all bets are off. We won't have a second to ourselves."

As much as she wanted Shelby to take her back to the shop and Rafael, Gisele couldn't disappoint her friend by ditching her now.

"You've been busy with your job. I've been working non-stop to get my business up and running and profitable." Gisele gave her friend an apologetic grimace. "Who has time for anything else?"

"Thing is, we need to *make* time for the people we care about." Shelby gave her a crooked smile. "I'm sorry if I've neglected our friendship. I promise to do better."

Gisele smiled at her friend, feeling guilty for wanting to be somewhere else. "Same. I'll do better."

Shelby pulled onto the road leading to the Crawdad Hole. The sun had sunk to the edge of the horizon, painting the sky brilliant shades of orange, mauve and magenta.

Determined to do her part as a friend, Gisele worked at keeping the conversation going. "So, how are you and Remy getting along?"

Shelby smiled. "He's great and so attentive. He anticipates my every move to the point he won't let me lift anything." Her lips twisted. "It's sweet and annoying at the same time. I'm pregnant, not an invalid."

"He cares and doesn't want you to hurt yourself," Gisele said.

"I know. I don't complain to him, but I secretly vacuum and mow the lawn when he's not at home."

Shelby grinned. "My lawn gets mowed twice a week. It's never looked better."

Gisele chuckled. "You're a stubborn, independent woman."

"I am. As are you." Shelby shot a pointed glance her way. "It's how we roll."

Sensing her friend was about to launch into questions she wasn't prepared to answer, Gisele brought the topic back to one Shelby was passionate about. "And the baby? Have you felt it kick?"

Shelby's face lit up. "I have. I'm convinced this little nugget is going to be a soccer player or a gymnast."

"Do you know what you're having?" Gisele asked, another stab of guilt hitting her in the gut. Shelby was her friend. A good friend would know the answers to her questions already.

Shelby shook her head. "Remy and I discussed it. We don't want to know until the day the baby is born."

Gisele groaned. "That's terrible. You're going to make us wait until you deliver? That's just cruel. That makes it hard to decorate at the baby shower. And where's the fun in gender-neutral baby clothes?"

Shelby chuckled. "I know. But we're sticking to the plan. We don't care if it's a boy or a girl. We'll love it either way. And if you don't want to get gender-neutral baby clothes, you can always get us stock in a disposable diaper company. I never realized just how many diapers a kid goes through in the first year of his life."

Gisele sighed. "You must be over the moon. You have a man who is crazy about you and a baby on the way. Life doesn't get better than that."

"It doesn't," Shelby agreed. "But what about you? When are you going to start dating again?"

Gisele stared out the window. "I was so busy renovating the shop and starting the business that I hadn't thought about it until recently." She shrugged. "I could be ready if the right guy asks me out." Her thoughts went to Rafael and what had almost happened on the floor of her shop. Heat flared at her core all over again.

"I'm glad you're thinking about it. You're young and beautiful. You deserve to find someone special. Just don't rush into anything. Know what you're getting into this time. Make sure you have the same values and expectations for a relationship. Get to know the guy before you consider having sex with him. Sex changes everything. Be picky. Know what you want, and don't settle for anything less."

Gisele had the feeling Shelby's warnings had to do with Rafael. Was she trying to protect her from the best-looking member of the team? Is that why she'd given Rafael the stink-eye?

It was sweet of Shelby to want to protect her from heartache, but Gisele wasn't as naïve as she was when she'd moved to New York City all those years ago.

She was a grown woman, had experienced betrayal and wouldn't fall for that kind of nonsense a second time around.

She was also in the prime of her life with needs beyond her battery-operated boyfriend, whose batteries had run out months ago.

Gisele sat up straighter and lifted her chin. "What if all I want is sex?" she asked. "It's been a while since I got laid. I might want to scratch my itch with no strings attached."

Shelby's head whipped around, and she almost ran off the road. "Are you kidding?"

Gisele reached for the steering wheel and gave it a little turn to keep them from driving into a ditch. "Sweetie, the road?"

"Got it." Shelby gripped the wheel and focused on keeping the SUV in her lane. Her lips pressed into a firm line. "You can't hit a person with a statement like that while she's driving."

"Sorry," Gisele said.

Shelby frowned. "You *are* kidding, right?"

Gisele shook her head. "No. I'm serious. Why is it okay for a man to sleep around before he marries and not okay if you're a woman?"

"I get what you're saying. Women have needs just like men. Committing to a long-term relationship isn't something you go into lightly. It has to be with the right person. Sometimes, it takes a while to find the one who fits. Who makes you complete."

"And how do you know it's the right person?" Gisele turned to Shelby. "How did you know Remy was the right one for you?"

Shelby's lips twisted. "I fell in love with him when he was dating my sister. He barely knew I existed. It wasn't until he came home after his military commitment was done that he finally saw *me*. As a woman, not a pesky kid tagging along with her sister. We were both different from when he was dating my sister, but deep down, we were the same."

"Wasn't it awkward that he'd dated your sister?" Gisele asked.

"Didn't bother me. And it doesn't bother Chrissy's husband. He got the girl in the long run. Now they have five kids and another on the way due around the same time as mine. They'll be cousins and grow up together." Shelby paused and grimaced. "That's not what you were asking."

No, it wasn't, but Shelby's face was flushed with the anticipation of welcoming her baby into a world filled with cousins to play with.

Gisele loved that her friend was so happy. Was she a little envious of that happiness? Absolutely.

"When Remy returned home from his time in the Navy, he finally knew I existed," Shelby said. "I made sure of that. The man aggravated the fire out of me. Sometimes, I didn't like him much. Hands down, I knew I could live without him. Did I want to? Hell no. So, how did I know he was the one for me?"

Shelby smiled softly and rested a hand on her belly. "The question isn't can I live without him? The real question I needed to ask myself was...do I *want* to live without him?"

Shelby parked in the gravel parking lot of the Crawdad Hole restaurant. They got out and picked their way across the loose gravel to the entrance.

The bouncer at the door gave a perfunctory glance at their driver's licenses and waved them inside. He knew who they were but he was a rule-follower.

Music vibrated throughout the room and in Gisele's ears. A jukebox in the corner supplied the tunes, with songs designed to make you cry in your beverage of choice—for most, that was beer—or kick up your heels in a lively two-step.

Shelby led the way to the bar and climbed onto one of the stools.

Gisele slid onto the stool beside her and started to order a beer. She thought about it and opted out. In deference to the pregnant woman, Gisele abstained from ordering an alcoholic beverage and settled on an ice-cold root beer.

Shelby eyed the bartender filling a mug with beer. "I'll be glad when this baby is out of my body, and I can enjoy a nice cold beer again." She ordered a ginger ale with a cherry on top and opened the food menu.

Gisele glanced over the list of sandwiches,

burgers and shellfish dishes the Crawdad Hole offered. Though she hadn't had lunch, nothing stood out on the menu. Because she didn't always like cooking for one, she'd eaten here and at other local restaurants and food trucks often enough to have gone through their menus. She would rather be seated across from Rafael, enjoying taco soup.

Shelby closed her menu and laid it on the counter. "I'm having the fried shrimp basket and a cup of their gumbo. What are you getting?"

"I'm not that hungry. I think I'll get a side salad and maybe an order of fried pickles we can share."

Shelby grinned. "Great. I love their fried pickles." She sat back in her seat and absently rubbed her hand over her belly.

"Is it hard being pregnant?" Gisele asked.

Her friend shrugged. "Yes and no. At first, I was tired a lot, and I couldn't stand certain smells—like diesel fumes. I'd throw up every time I smelled diesel fumes. That was all in the first trimester. Once my body adjusted to the parasite growing inside, it's been pretty easy. I do have to pee more often, and that will only get worse the bigger the baby grows. All in all, I'm okay so far. Ask me that question when I'm as big as a house and can't see my feet anymore." Shelby laughed, her face flushing with happiness. "Is it crazy that I'm looking forward to that stage?"

"Of course you are. It'll mean you're that much closer to meeting your baby." Gisele's heart swelled with love and happiness for her friend as she moved into a different phase of her life. Having grown up as the granddaughter of the Voodoo Queen, Gisele always thought the only way to find that level of happiness would be to leave her weird world behind.

She had left and found that the grass wasn't always greener outside the bayou, weird wasn't a bad thing and the men weren't any better in New York City. When she'd come home to Bayou Mambaloa, she'd told herself she could be content to live her life alone. For the past three years, that had been true.

Until a group of former military special operations guys moved in and changed everything.

Shelby glanced around the room. "Those people are leaving. Let's take their table. I can't get comfortable on this bar stool."

They carried their drinks to the table where Danielle French, the waitress, was clearing the empty mugs and bottles.

"Hey, Danny," Shelby greeted the woman. "How are you holding up with the festival in town?"

Danny glanced up and smiled. "Other than sore feet, I'm doing fine. I've made more in tips these past few days than I do all month. No complaints here." She lifted her chin toward Gisele. "Hey, girl. I heard you had a break-in last night. I'm so sorry it happened to you and your shop. Things like that leave you feeling punchy for a long time. I'd hate to sleep there after that. If you need a place to stay for a while, I have a spare bedroom in my trailer. You're welcome to have it for as long as you need it."

Gisele was touched by Danny's offer. The woman could barely afford her rent and utilities. Having an extra person living with her would be a financial strain. Yet, she'd offered to share her trailer with no mention of splitting rent or contributing in any way.

Gisele recognized how blessed she was to live in a community where people who had very little would share down to their last slice of bread. "Thank you, Danny. I really appreciate your offer, but I'll stay in my apartment. I'm going to have a security system installed. I'll be all right."

She lifted her heavy tray onto her shoulder without losing a single mug or bottle. "The offer stands. All you have to do is call. I'll help you move your stuff."

"Thanks," Gisele repeated.

Danny left with the empties and returned a few minutes later with their order.

Shelby consumed her cup of gumbo first and then dove into the basket of fried shrimp. "Help yourself. There's enough here for two people."

Gisele ate fried pickles and half of her salad, sipping on root beer while thinking about Rafael.

Occupied with eating for two, Shelby didn't try to carry on a conversation until she'd satisfied her appetite and sat back, rubbing her stomach. "Better," she said, her gaze going to Gisele's relatively untouched salad. "What's wrong?"

Gisele met Shelby's intense gaze with a cocked eyebrow. "Who says anything is wrong?"

Shelby waved a hand toward Gisele's salad. "You haven't eaten enough to keep your bird alive. Is something bothering you?" She laid down her fork and leaned forward. "I'm here. Talk."

When Gisele hesitated, Shelby's brow dipped low. "Is it Rafael? Are you having sex with him?"

Gisele gasped. "Shelby." She glanced around the bar and grill. Typical of Shelby, she didn't mince words. Instead, she went straight to the heart. "Seriously?" Gisele lowered her voice to a whisper. "You're going to broadcast my love life, or lack of one, in a crowded room?"

"I didn't broadcast. I asked a question in a normal tone of voice." She pointed a finger at Gisele. "You didn't answer." Her eyes narrowed and then widened. "You *are* having sex with him. I knew it. I told Remy to warn him off you. Rafael is not the man for you."

Gisele sat back in her seat. "Since when do you make decisions about the men I sleep with?"

Shelby crossed her arms over her chest. "Since you came back to Bayou Mambaloa with your tail between your legs, all butt hurt because some asshole broke your heart."

"I didn't come back to Bayou Mambaloa because of a broken heart. I came back because I wanted to come back where I had friends and family I could trust." Gisele glared at one of those friends. "At least, I thought I could trust them. Now, here you are telling me who I can date or not date." She lifted her chin. "And why shouldn't I date Rafael?"

"We were talking about sleeping with him. Trust me. He's not the guy for you." Shelby's expression softened. "He's vowed never to marry or commit to a woman. The man goes out with a girl a couple of times and then moves on to his next conquest."

"So?" Gisele said. "Who said I was looking for a ring? I like being single. I don't have to pick up after or cook for anyone else. I set my own schedule without having to consult or compromise. I like my life."

"Then why the interest in Rafael?" Shelby asked.

Gisele raised her hands, palms up. "Why not? If he's not into marriage and signing up for the long haul...good. Neither am I. Not everyone lucks into the kind of love you and Remy share. I'm not pining over the fact I don't have someone who worships the ground I walk on. Why is it so hard to believe I'm happy with my life? I'm happy, damn it."

Shelby frowned, "If you're so happy, why are you so insistent you're happy? It's like you're trying to convince yourself."

Gisele rolled her head back and stared at the ceiling for a second before turning her gaze back on her friend. "I'm fine. I learned a valuable lesson the first time around. Never relinquish control of your heart to anyone."

"I just don't want you hurt again," Shelby said, her eyes filling with tears. She brushed them away, muttering, "Damned hormones."

Gisele reached across the table and took Shelby's hand. "I appreciate that you want to protect me, but you can't tell me who I can and can't see or sleep with. I'm a grown woman. I can make my own decisions and my own mistakes. That's how we learn."

"He won't stay," Shelby repeated.

"So what?" Gisele said. "Maybe I'll be the one to leave him with a broken heart. Would you be as concerned for him?"

Shelby stared into Gisele's eyes for a long moment. "Be careful, Gisele. I love you like a sister. Rafael's not a bad man. He's actually very funny, nice and good at what he does. He's completely loyal to his team and would do anything for them."

"Sounds perfect," Gisele said.

"It's his track record with women that's abysmal. Gisele, don't become another notch on his bedpost." She sat back and let out a sigh. "Whew. That was hard. I'm not all that good at this touchy-feely stuff. It takes a lot out of me."

It was taking a lot out of Gisele, as well.

Shelby gave her a tight smile. "Now that I've got that off my chest, have you tasted the peach cobbler?

Want to share an order and save me from eating the whole piece by myself?"

Gisele shook her head. "Not me. I'm not really hungry."

Shelby nodded. "I really don't need cobbler, either." She smothered a yawn. "What I do need is to go to bed. I got up for the early shift this morning. I'm tired."

"Me, too," Gisele said.

"Would it hurt your feelings if we called it a night?" Shelby yawned again. "Girl time isn't what it used to be, is it? How did we ever stay up all night giggling?"

"I don't know. Now, if I stay up past midnight, I'm worthless all the next day." She waved a hand at Danny, who hurried over.

"What can I get you two?" Danny asked.

"Could I get a to-go box for my salad? And we'd like to pay the bill." Gisele handed her credit card to the waitress.

"Gotcha." Danny took the card with a smile. "I'll be right back."

Shelby frowned. "I was going to buy *your* dinner."

"You can next time," Gisele promised.

Shelby's brow puckered. "Will there be a next time? Have I crossed the line and ruined our friendship?" She stared across the table at Gisele. "That's the last thing I wanted to do. I love you like a sister. I should've flown my ass up to New York City to put the hurt on the man who did you wrong. He shouldn't have gotten away with ruining your career and breaking your heart."

Gisele laid her hand over Shelby's. "Our friendship is intact. And don't worry about New York. He did me a favor and showed his true colors. That whole situation opened my eyes to what really matters."

Shelby turned her hand over and squeezed Gisele's. "Family and friends?"

"Exactly," Gisele said. "I didn't come home with my tail between my legs. I came home to the people and place I love. It wasn't my last resort. It was my first choice."

Danny returned with Gisele's credit card, receipt and a box for the salad she never ate.

"Thank you, Danny." Gisele took the card, signed the bill and dumped her salad into the box. She looked across the table at Shelby, whose eyelids struggled to remain open. "Let's get you home."

Gisele wanted Shelby to drop her off at the end of Main Street, insisting she could walk the rest of the way to her shop.

Shelby refused and drove her all the way.

"Are you going to stay awake long enough to drive yourself home?" Gisele asked as she unbuckled her seatbelt in front of her shop.

"I'll be fine. I've pulled enough night shifts; I can

drive the streets of Bayou Mambaloa with my eyes closed."

Gisele's hand froze on the belt buckle.

Shelby laughed. "I'm kidding. But you should have seen the look on your face. I'll wait for you to get inside and then drive straight home. With my eyes open."

Still, Gisele hesitated, worried her friend was too sleepy to make it across their small town to her cottage.

Shelby touched her arm. "Go. I'll be fine. Remy just texted me. He's at home waiting for me."

Gisele met Shelby's gaze. "Thank you for making me go to dinner with you. We need to do Girl Time again. Soon."

"Next time, we should include Bernie, Felina and Ouida Mae."

"Don't forget Camille and Amelia," Gisele said.

"Them, too." Shelby waved a hand. "Guard your heart, my friend."

"I've got this," she assured her friend. As she walked away, she wondered if she really did.

She'd only spent a short amount of time with the man.

Shelby had fallen in love with Remy long before they became a couple. She'd dated douchebag in New York for months before she'd trusted him enough to sleep with him—and look where that had gotten her.

Having only spent a few hours with Rafael, surely her heart wasn't anywhere near at risk.

Was it?

CHAPTER 9

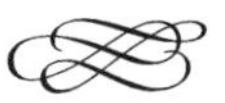

GISELE CARRIED her boxed salad to the front door of her shop and looked to see if Rafael had installed one of the little alarms on this one. It faced the street and had a streetlight directly in front of the door. Anyone who attempted to enter would risk being seen. She really didn't need a screeching alarm on this door.

She unlocked the deadbolt, held her breath and pushed open the door, waiting for the alarm to shriek like a flight of banshees.

When it didn't, she let go of the breath and walked inside. Good, he hadn't installed an alarm on the front, just the back and the windows.

The shop was as neat, if not neater than when she'd left it. The mango she'd flung when she'd tripped was at the bottom of Johnny's cage, almost completely consumed. The lettuce leaf had been shredded, and much of it had been eaten.

Johnny whistled and moved from side to side on his upper perch, repeating *Cheeky bastard* several times before whistling again.

"Did he feed you the mango and lettuce?" she asked.

Johnny's head bobbed up and down. *He's a keeper,* he squawked. *Cheeky bastard.*

Gisele laughed. "Yes, to both, my good man." Although Shelby wouldn't agree. She leaned closer to the cage and whispered, "She's worried he'll break my heart."

Johnny squawked loudly.

"I know, right?" Gisele lifted her chin. "She should be more worried about me breaking Rafael's heart. I suspect someone has done it once for him to swear off women."

Her stomach rumbled, reminding her she hadn't had much to eat since the éclair Rafael had given her that morning.

The man had done more for her in the past twenty-four hours than any date had in the past.

So, he wasn't into commitment. They could be friends, couldn't they?

Friends with benefits?

Heat burned through her and coiled at her core at the thought of those benefits.

She looked down at the box of salad in her hand, an idea forming. Shelby's warning about Rafael flew out the window.

Before she could talk herself out of it, she walked back through the front door, locked it and marched across the alley and up the stairs to Rafael's apartment.

After she knocked on the door, regrets bubbled up to the surface.

She turned to run.

The door behind her opened. Rafael stood there wearing nothing but a pair of gym shorts and a towel draped over his shoulder. Droplets of water fell from his hair onto his bare chest, making Gisele's mouth go dry.

"Gisele, I didn't expect you back so soon."

She held up her box of salad. "Is the offer of taco soup still open?"

He grinned. "Of course. Come in."

"I brought a salad if you're into rabbit food."

His chuckle did crazy things to Gisele's insides. "I eat an occasional salad. A body needs roughage, or so my doctor says."

Gisele entered Rafael's apartment, looking around at empty boxes, flattened and leaning against the wall. The small living room contained a black leather couch and a white marble coffee table with a stack of books on it.

Off the kitchenette was a dinette table with a bright red lacquered top and metal rim that could have been straight out of the nineteen fifties. It sported two metal chairs, the seats covered in equally bright red vinyl.

Rafael closed the door behind her and hurried past her. "My sofa and coffee table came today. The dining table was here. Between what you see and my bed, that's all the furniture. Not that there's room for much more."

"What? No television?" She cocked an eyebrow.

He grinned. "It's on order. I like to watch football." He ducked into the only bedroom. "Are you a fan?"

Of him, yes. Of football? "I watch the occasional New Orleans Saints game at the Crawdad Hole with friends. I'm not what you'd consider a rabid fan, though I enjoy an exciting game. I've never participated in Fantasy Football, though I'd like to understand what the fuss is all about." She peered into his bedroom, where a king-sized bed took up most of the room. He'd made it up with charcoal gray sheets and a black fuzzy blanket.

Gisele's pulse spun up, sending hot blood throughout her body, culminating low in her belly.

Rafael rummaged in a duffel bag, finally pulling out a T-shirt. "We'll have to indoctrinate you into the legions of foaming-at-the-mouth fandom."

"I'd like that. I need a new hobby."

"Isn't dabbling in Voodoo interesting enough?"

She shrugged. "Everyone expects that of me. I grew up resisting their expectations. I wanted to be like everyone else."

Rafael tossed the towel in the corner and pulled the T-shirt over his head and down his broad chest and washboard abs.

Gisele's breath lodged in her throat. She wanted him to take the T-shirt back off. No. She wanted to take the T-shirt off him and run her hands over all that sexy, taut skin with the hard muscles beneath.

Girl. Get a grip.

She tore her gaze away from Rafael and wandered into the kitchenette, putting distance between herself and all that gorgeous manhood before she made a pass at him.

Shelby's warnings played like a recording on an infinite loop. "He will never commit. He has sex with a woman a couple of times and moves on. Don't lose your heart to a man like that."

The man Shelby had warned her about strode toward her with a smile that could melt the sturdiest of knees. "I take it you came straight over since I don't hear the sound of sirens screeching, unless you went through the front door of the shop."

Gisele nodded, afraid to trust her voice to do more than squeak. She swallowed and said, "Front door only."

"Good. I need to show you how to disarm the alarms should they be set off. I'll do that after we have that taco soup I promised."

Gisele's move into the kitchenette to put distance between her and him backfired. He joined her in the small space and leaned around her to open the refrigerator door, effectively trapping her, his arm brushing across her breast.

An electric charge shot through her, making her gasp softly.

Rafael's brow furrowed as he stared down at her, the refrigerator door open, pouring out cool air over Gisele's hot skin. "Are you okay?" he asked.

She shook her head. "Yes."

His chuckle made her body burn even hotter.

"You're shaking head says no, but your mouth is saying yes. Which is it?"

She raised a hand to her chest in a futile attempt to slow her racing heartbeat. "Yes and no."

He nodded, his brow puckering. "*Okaayy*. That's much clearer. Am I making you uncomfortable?"

She nodded.

Immediately, he tensed and stepped back. "I'm sorry. I don't mean to make you feel uncomfortable."

Her hand shot out to grab his arm. "I didn't say I didn't like it."

His lips twitched. "I'm not sure what you're saying. It sounds like double talk."

She sighed. "What I mean to say is...yes, you make me uncomfortable, but in a good way."

His dark pupils flared. For a long moment, he stared down into her eyes without moving. Then he reached into the refrigerator, pulled out a container and set it on the counter. Away from her.

With his back to her, he worked silently at spooning taco soup from the container into a bowl.

Wasn't he going to say anything? She'd more or less admitted that she was sexually attracted to him. Hell, she'd shown him that she was when she'd groped him in her shop earlier.

He'd groped back. Her breast still tingled from where he'd cupped it beneath her shirt.

Why the hell was he pulling away?

She reached out and touched his back.

Rafael froze, the spoon hovering over the bowl of soup.

Anger bubbled up inside Gisele. "Why am I getting insanely mixed signals from you? Have I done something that you don't like?"

He shook his head. "Just the opposite," he murmured.

"You like it when I touch you?" She ran her hand down his back. "But you won't turn and look me in the eye. I don't get it." Gisele stomped her foot. "Rafael, talk to me!"

Rafael spun to face Gisele.

Her eyes flashed fire, and her cheeks were a pretty flushed pink. She was so beautiful that he had to clench his fists to keep from pulling her into his arms.

"Did you and Shelby talk?" he asked.

Her eyes narrowed. "Yes. That's what friends do when they have dinner together."

"Did my name come into the conversation?" He captured her gaze with his and held it.

Gisele was first to look away. "Yes."

"She's right, you know," he said softly.

Her gaze swung back to his. "Right about what?"

"You shouldn't get involved with me," he said, Valentin's words still stinging. "I'm not right for you."

Gisele's eyes widened. "Is that what she told you?"

"Not directly," he admitted. "Through an elected representative of so-called teammates."

Gisele clapped a hand over her mouth. "Seriously? Are all our friends ganging up on us to keep us apart?" She pulled her phone out of her skirt pocket. "I have a few things to say to them about that."

Rafael covered her hand before she could call anyone. "They're doing it out of love. They're worried about you."

"I can make up my own mind. I don't need well-intentioned do-gooders telling me who I can or can't have sex with."

His lip slid up in a grin and then turned downward. "The thing is, you should listen to your friend. I'm not the kind of guy who's looking for a happily-ever-after. I will never marry, settle down in a little house and have a handful of children." He turned back to the bowl of soup, opened the microwave and placed it inside. "I'm not boyfriend, fiancé or husband material. If that's what you're looking for, run the other way." He poked buttons on the control panel with more force than was necessary, holding his breath.

He fully expected Gisele to leave. A part of him hoped she would. It would be easier if she did. Another part of him wanted her to stay, get naked and make love with him until the sun came up and the gossips spread word through the little town that they'd spent the night together.

He stared at the bowl on the microwave turntable as it went around and around, like his thoughts. Should he pursue Gisele? Or should he do what half of Bayou Mambaloa wanted him to do and steer clear? "What do you want?" he asked, his voice raspy as he pushed words past his constricted vocal cords.

"I want people to quit making my decision for me. I want to have the choice of who I'm with without interference from well-meaning busybodies."

A hand settled on his back; light fingers stroked from his shoulder down to his waist.

Fire spread from where she touched, burning through every cell in Rafael's body. He tensed, ready to spin and take her into his arms.

"They might be right," Gisele said softly. "It might be a mistake for us to be together. You might decide to walk away at any moment. But what I want right now..." Gisele paused.

Rafael held his breath, waiting for her next word, praying it was the one he wanted to hear.

Gisele leaned into him, pressing her breasts to his back, her arms circling his waist. "I want—"

The microwave beeped, and the turntable came to a halt.

Gisele pressed her forehead against his back. "We can*not* catch a single break." Her body shook gently, then harder.

Was she crying?

He disengaged her arms from around his waist and turned. When he tipped her chin up and stared down into her moist eyes, his heart pinched hard in his chest.

Then, the source of her body's tremors emerged in a stifled chuckle. She laughed, tears spilling from her eyes.

Her chuckles and laughter were contagious.

Soon, Rafael was laughing with her.

"I almost busted a gut when Shelby told you your barn door was open." Gisele wiped the tears from her eyes.

"Your sexy walk had me ready to tackle you," he said, brushing her hair back behind her ear. "Until you crashed."

"I can't believe we almost made love on the floor of the shop." Gisele shook her head. "In broad daylight."

He tipped her chin up and stared down into her

eyes. "And we would have if I hadn't left the back door open."

"I doubt a closed door would've stopped her," Gisele's lips twisted in a wry smile. "She was on a mission."

"To warn you off me." Rafael sighed and rested his forehead against hers. "You're an independent woman with a smart and beautiful head on your shoulders. I can't promise you anything but today. Now. The present. I won't lie and tell you different, just to get you in my bed. You can choose to walk away or tell me to leave you alone. I don't want to...but I'll respect your wishes." He lifted his head and met her gaze. "What do you want, Gisele?"

She smiled up at him. "I want you."

His heart sang at her words. He hadn't expected the rush of joy that filled him so completely. He tempered his elation with a warning. "If we're together today, we might not be tomorrow."

She lifted a shoulder and let it fall. "So, tomorrow is not a given. You might decide being with me is not for you. It goes both ways. I might decide you're not who I want. Either way, we walk away. No strings. No hard feelings." She held out her hand. "Deal?"

Rafael's brow wrinkled. He'd always been the one to walk away ever since his fiancée had walked away from him. How would he feel if Gisele was the one who ended it?

One of her eyebrows rose on her forehead,

though her hand still hovered between them. “Do we have a deal, or have you decided to opt out of this before it starts?”

He wasn’t going to walk away now. But her comment about him not being right for her had him stymied.

Her face softened into a gentle smile. Gisele reached up to cup his face and rose onto her toes to brush her lips across his. “What do you want, Rafael?”

Every wall inside Rafael cracked, and the emotions he’d held back for so long rushed through like water pushing through cracks in a dam. He had no way to stop the flow, to plug the holes. If he kissed her now, there was no going back.

He crushed her to him and lowered his mouth to hers. “I want you,” he said and then kissed her.

CHAPTER 10

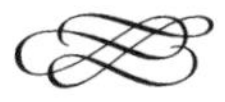

GISELE OPENED TO HIS KISS, meeting his tongue with hers in a long, slow caress that left her breathless and wanting more.

They weren't in her shop; the sun had gone down hours ago. No one would come knocking on Rafael's door.

Nothing stood in the way of the inevitable.

Her body quivered in anticipation.

They were going to make love.

When she thought she might never need to breathe again, Rafael raised his head.

Then he bent, swept her up into his arms and carried her the few short steps across his apartment into his bedroom.

She cupped his cheeks between her palms and kissed him gently as he lowered her feet to the ground.

As soon as her feet settled on the floor, he tugged her shirt from the waistband of her skirt and raised it up her body and over her head. He tossed it over his shoulder and reached for the clasp on her skirt.

Gisele grabbed the hem of the T-shirt he'd just put on and dragged it upward.

He took over and yanked it over his head. It sailed across the room to join her shirt. Somewhere.

The rest of their clothes disappeared in an instant.

Once again, Rafael scooped her up in his arms and kissed her. Then he laid her gently onto the crisp gray sheets.

He dropped onto the mattress beside her and brushed a finger across her lips. As that finger drifted across her chin and down the length of her neck, he lowered his head and claimed her mouth in a slow, sensuous kiss.

Gisele had always felt a little self-conscious with her last boyfriend. He'd always made disparaging comments about other men and women, criticizing their bodies, hair, intelligence or anything he found less than perfect in his eyes.

When she'd gotten naked with him, and his gaze had raked over her body, she'd felt like she'd come up short every time. Near the end of their relationship, she'd gotten to where she'd turned off the lights before she'd taken off her clothes. Then, he hadn't seen faults to silently judge her.

Rafael left the lights on in the bedroom. As he

kissed his way down her neck, his hand preceded his lips and captured one of her breasts in his palm.

He leaned back, his gaze sweeping over her.

Gisele held her breath, shrinking inside, wishing the light wasn't shining down on every one of her flaws from hips too broad to breasts that were too small.

Rafael's gaze came back up to hers, his eyes shining. "You are beautiful."

She shook her head. "My breasts are too small, and my hips too broad."

His lips spread in a grin as he weighed one breast in his hand. "Nope. Your breast fits perfectly in my palm. Besides, any more than a mouthful is a waste." He winked and bent to kiss the tip of the one he held. Then he sucked it into his mouth and flicked the nipple until it hardened into a tight rosy button.

A moan rose in her throat. Gisele writhed beneath him, her body responding to his touch. Her breathing grew ragged as he moved to the other breast and treated it to the same tender attention as he'd given the first.

Gisele wove her hands into his hair, holding him close, urging him to take more and wanting to be closer.

He sucked her nipple into his mouth and pulled gently, teasing the nipple with the tip of his tongue.

When he abandoned her breast, she could breathe again. But not for long. His mouth trailed down her torso, pressing kisses to each of her ribs, his tongue dipping into her bellybutton as his fingers slid further south to the apex of her thighs.

Gisele's breath hitched when he parted her folds and stroked her sex. A long, coarse finger dipped into her channel and swirled. Another finger joined it.

Rafael worked his way down her body, parted her legs and lay down between them. He draped first one thigh and then the other over his shoulders.

Then he parted her folds with his thumbs and touched his tongue to her clit.

"Oh, Rafael." Gisele's hips rose off the mattress.

He chuckled, his breath warm against her sex. "Like that?"

"Yessss!" She hissed when he flicked her clit and then swirled his tongue around it slowly, gently, growing more and more intense with each round. At the same time, he slid three fingers into her channel, moving them in and out in the same rhythm as his tongue moved against her clit.

Gisele forgot how to breathe as her body tensed like a bowstring pulled to its limit.

All it would take would be one last flick...

Rafael expertly tapped her there, setting off an explosion of sensations that radiated from the point of contact, spreading at lightning speed through her body to the very tips of her fingers and toes.

He didn't let up the pressure, continuing the strokes and thrusts, giving it everything.

Gisele grasped his hair and called out, "Oh, sweet peaches...Yes!"

Her heels dug into the mattress as she rode the current all the way to the very end.

She collapsed back against the sheets, sucking air into her lungs. "I've...never...felt like...that before."

Rafael chuckled as he climbed up her body and settled his hips between her legs. "And that was just foreplay." He pressed a swift kiss to her lips, his mouth musky from her sex. "Your opinion of foreplay? Overrated?"

"Noooo. So underrated. Absolutely essential." She grasped his buttocks in her hands and pulled him closer until his cock nudged her entrance. "Satisfying. But not nearly enough." She urged him closer.

"Wait," he said and leaned over to the nightstand, pulled out a drawer and fished out a condom.

Thank goodness he was thinking. She had yet to come down from the throes of her orgasm to even consider protection.

He came up on his knees, tore open the packet and removed the condom.

Gisele took it from his hand and rolled it down his engorged staff to the base. She lingered there, fondling his balls and liking how he sucked in a breath and held it.

"Enough," he growled and dropped down to lean over her on his arms.

"What do you want, Rafael," she asked, smoothing a hand over his tight ass.

"To be inside you," he said and bent to kiss her, his tongue sliding between her teeth as his cock slipped into her moist channel.

She'd loved how he'd brought her so effortlessly to orgasm, but this...

Gisele raised her knees and lifted her hips, her hands pulling him closer, deeper. When he was all the way inside her, his balls warm against her anus, she held him there for a long moment, letting her body adjust to his size.

He didn't rush her, letting her choose when she was ready. Gisele eased him out, his shaft sliding easily all the way to the tip before she reversed course and brought him back in.

Back out and back in, she moved him, increasing speed and force with each pass.

His body was tense with his effort to control his movements.

When she reached a certain speed, or maybe Rafael lost control...whatever happened, Rafael took over.

Gisele released her hold on his ass and gripped the bedsheets, rising to meet his thrusts, her breaths coming in short, ragged gasps as she neared another climax.

He thrust deeper and faster until he slammed home one last time, sending Gisele over the edge for the second time. Her channel convulsed around his length as his cock pulsed his release.

Gisele threw back her head, her body drained, her soul satisfied and her libido sated...for the moment. She drew in a deep breath and let it out slowly. "Wow."

Rafael dropped low, kissed her, and then rolled them both onto their sides without losing their intimate connection. "Amazing."

She nodded. Words seemed inadequate. With the afterglow fading quickly, her thoughts went back to all Shelby had said about Rafael, his vow to himself never to marry, and how he left each woman before she had a chance to fall in love with him. Her gut knotted. Was she too late? Was the knot in her belly a clear indication she was already grieving the loss of Rafael? She hadn't even left his apartment, yet she was in a downward spiral of depression. She wanted to stay with him. Not just for today. Gisele wanted tomorrow, the next day and the ones after that.

Shelby's warning echoed in Gisele's head. *He won't commit, refuses to marry and doesn't date a woman for long.*

But how long? A day, a week? She was torn between staying for however long he would allow and running back to her apartment. How had she let her heart be drawn in by him, knowing he wasn't a forever kind of guy? He'd been crystal clear. She'd known his limitations upfront.

His friends had warned him to stay away from her. Her friend had warned her of his drawbacks. Yet, Gisele had ignored those warnings, claiming she could handle it, and walked right into Rafael's arms and bed.

With sanity returning, she had the sudden and urgent need to go back to her place. Only space away from Rafael and time would help her sort through her feelings to allow herself to make better decisions. She had to leave or stay and go for round two… "When can we do that again?" she asked.

Rafael laughed. "Are you ready now?"

"No," she said. "I'm just curious how long it takes you to recover."

He pulled her into his arms and nuzzled her neck. "Long enough."

She kissed him once more, savoring what might be her last taste of him. Then she pushed his arms away and rolled out of the bed.

A frown formed on Rafael's forehead. "Where are you going?"

She gave him a confused look. "Back to my apartment, of course."

His frown deepened. "Why?"

"You need time to recover, and I need sleep." She gave him a quick smile. "I don't want you to think I'm clingy or want anything more than great sex." She found her bra, skirt and shirt, but couldn't locate her panties. She gave up looking for them and slipped her shirt over her head. After stepping into her skirt, she pulled it up over her hips and fastened the catch.

"You're really going?"

Gisele nodded. "I really am."

Rafael sat up in the bed and crossed his arms over his chest. "Are you being sarcastic or somehow testing me?"

She moved toward the door of his bedroom, edging slowly toward escape. "Neither. You said so yourself that you're not into commitment."

"Yes, but that doesn't mean I'll kick you out of my place immediately after."

"You're only into today," she reminded him softly. "Tomorrow has no guarantees. You'll be happy to know, I'm not holding you to anything. No demands. I won't manipulate you with guilt or expect anything from you beyond the moment. I assume it goes both ways. Equal opportunity and all." She gave him a tight smile.

"What if I want you to stay?" Rafael asked.

"Specific amounts of time could be construed as bleeding into the future. It requires you to commit to a certain timeframe that isn't now. Can you be specific about how long you want me to stay?"

"I don't know. I thought we'd cuddle for a while."

"Is a while equivalent to an hour?" Why was she still standing there when her chest was tight, and her knees were shaking? "It doesn't matter. I'm going to my apartment.

Gisele really hadn't thought through her need to leave. She just couldn't stay the night with him. Every moment she spent with Rafael made her increasingly aware of how she'd feel when he walked away.

Shitty, depressed and bone-achingly lonely.

She'd be better off cutting it off before she sank even further into feelings for the man.

"I have to go," she murmured, spinning on her bare heels.

She walked out of his bedroom. As soon as she was out of his sight, she ran for the exit. She flung open the door and darted outside and down the metal stairs.

She was halfway down the staircase when a loud shrieking sound cut through the night.

Gisele froze, her gaze shooting toward the rear of the shop. The alarm kept screaming. A dark figure ran away from the back of her building, disappearing into the night.

Footsteps pounded on the staircase above where Gisele stood. She looked up to see Rafael, wearing the gym shorts, barefooted and carrying a handgun, as he raced down the stairs toward her.

As he passed her, he called out, "Get back in my apartment and lock the door."

When she didn't move immediately, he barked, "Now!"

Gisele jumped and ran up to his apartment. As she passed through his open door, she looked back.

Rafael reached the bottom of the staircase, turned and sprinted across the alley toward the back of the shop and disappeared.

Her heart leaped into her throat. She stood for a long moment framed in the doorway, every fiber of her being screaming for her to go after him.

What if the man who'd tried to break into her building was armed? What if he was lying in wait to take Rafael down?

What if Rafael was attacked, shot or stabbed? He could bleed out before anyone got to him.

Gisele's heart banged hard against her ribs as she stood there, every horrible scenario playing out in her mind.

No way. She couldn't hide in his apartment when he might be injured.

She had run back down the stairs and crossed the alley when a figure emerged from the back of her building.

A stab of fear ripped through her, and a scream rose in her throat.

The figure emerged into the starlight.

Gisele clapped a hand over her mouth to stifle her scream and staggered forward into Rafael's arms.

He wrapped his arms around her and held her close, his handgun bumping against her back. "I told you to go back into my apartment," he said with his lips pressed to the top of her head. He turned her toward the stairs. "Come on. Let's get you back inside." He pressed his empty hand to the small of her back and guided her back to his building and up the stairs.

"What about Johnny?" Gisele asked as they reached the door to his apartment. She turned to go back down, but his hand blocked her.

"He's fine," Rafael said. "I checked in on him. The intruder didn't get past the door. The alarm scared him off. It did its job."

Gisele let Rafael usher her through the door.

Once inside, she stood, looking around, her brow furrowed, at a loss for what to do now.

Rafael made a 911 call and reported the attempted break-in. A deputy would investigate.

"They probably won't find anything," Rafael said as he ended the call.

"Why is this happening?" Gisele looked up into Rafael's eyes. "My shop isn't anything special. I don't keep a lot of cash lying around. I don't understand."

Rafael pulled her into his arms and held her. "I don't know what's going on, but I know one thing for certain."

Gisele laid her cheek against his chest, listening to the reassuring beat of his heart. "What do you know?"

"You're not staying over there. Not until we figure out who the hell is trying to get in and why."

As much as she wanted to argue with the man, she couldn't.

As fiercely independent as she liked to think she was, she wasn't stupid. She couldn't deal with the situation by herself. Having someone with combat and self-defense skills would come in handy and maybe keep her alive.

When she'd left his apartment a few minutes earlier, she'd been running scared—not of Rafael, but of her growing feelings for the man.

She'd nearly lost her shit when he'd disappeared going after the intruder.

In that moment, she'd realized what she was afraid to admit. The reason she'd left his apartment. The one thing that would surely put an earlier end to whatever was happening between her and Rafael.

She'd realized that though she might be able to live with the man...

She couldn't live without him.

In the few hours she'd spent with Rafael, she'd fallen under his spell, succumbed to his charm and landed head over heels for the cheeky bastard.

CHAPTER 11

IT TOOK SOME CONVINCING, but Rafael finally got Gisele back in his bed.

Not to make love but to try to sleep when sleep was the furthest thing from their minds.

Someone wanted inside the Mamba Wamba gift shop. Two attempts had been made, and the sheriff's department didn't have a single clue that would lead them to the culprit.

Rafael lay awake well into the early hours of the morning, holding Gisele as she slept fitfully. In his mind, he'd gone through every possible suspect he could think of, which didn't even amount to a handful of people. Who would target the gift shop and why? And if it wasn't the gift shop, who would target Gisele? She was one of the kindest, most giving people he knew.

Was her connection with the bayou's Voodoo queen enough of a reason to terrorize her?

Rafael drifted into a light sleep, remaining aware enough to come up fighting should a threat present itself.

He must have slept harder than he'd thought. A soft sound dragged him out of REM sleep to fully awake in a split second. He sat up in the bed and reached for the gun on the nightstand. His gaze swept through what he could see in the room outside the bedroom door.

The colorful swirl of a skirt flitted by.

Rafael left the bed and crept toward the door. As he reached it, Gisele appeared in front of him, a coffee mug filled to the brim cradled in one hand.

She smiled, her face a little rosier than when she'd gone to sleep the night before, but dark smudges under her eyes gave testament to troubled sleep. "Good morning. Here." She handed the coffee mug to him and pointed to the small table. "Sit. I'm making breakfast."

"You don't have to make my breakfast," he said. "I should make yours."

She shrugged. "You brought me breakfast yesterday when you delivered the éclair. If I cook your breakfast this morning, we can call it even. Either way, I'm having eggs." She spun and returned to the kitchenette, making busy noises as she opened and closed drawers and doors in pursuit of a pan, spatula and cooking spray.

Rafael didn't have a lot of kitchenware, which was okay, considering there wasn't much room in the small space. What he had, he'd unpacked the day before and stowed in various cabinets.

His landlord, YaYa, had gifted him with a basket of basic staples to welcome him to the apartment. Otherwise, his refrigerator would have only contained one beer short of a sixpack and the taco soup he'd thrown together from cans of beans and the hamburger meat he'd picked up at Broussard's Country Store.

Among the items YaYa had left in the gift basket was a carton of fresh farm eggs, a small package of custom ground, dry roast coffee, a small jar of homemade apple butter and a loaf of bread from the bakery. All items were from local sources, with their labels clearly displayed.

Rafael liked that she'd given him a taste of Bayou Mambaloa. Some of the items were from places he had yet to try. He'd felt more a part of the community than just an outsider holing up at the boarding house.

Now, with Gisele standing barefoot in the kitchen with her hair pulled back in a loose ponytail anchored at the base of her neck, he was even more thankful for the gift. It meant they didn't have to go out to eat breakfast. He would have more "alone" time with this woman.

Since he'd been jilted, he'd avoided having a woman stay the night at his place. He'd go to the woman's home and leave in the middle of the night. Staying gave the impression he would be around longer than a one-night stand. He hadn't wanted to give any woman a reason to believe he'd stick around when he'd been upfront with them about no commitment.

But here he was, the morning after, watching the quirky Voodoo shop owner standing there in her flowy, colorful skirt, her bare feet peeking out from beneath the hem—and he liked it. In fact, he could get used to seeing her every morning.

His gut twisted into a tight knot.

After they'd made love last night, she'd walked out of his apartment. If the alarm hadn't gone off when it had, she'd have gone home to her place.

Like he'd done to so many women in the past few years. Like he'd more or less warned Gisele he'd do to her.

His stomach roiled.

God, he was a bastard.

Gisele glanced up with a smile. "How do you like your eggs?"

"Over easy," he responded automatically, though he wasn't the least bit hungry. What he needed was to go for a run. Maybe that would help loosen the knot twisting inside.

Then again, he was afraid that if he went for a

run, he'd keep running until he was too far to return. Only, he couldn't leave Gisele alone. He was responsible for protecting her.

He could take Landry up on his offer to switch places. Rafael could go to the New Orleans job, and Landry would look after Gisele.

The thought of leaving someone else in charge of Gisele's safety made that knot in his belly twist even tighter. If he went to New Orleans, he wouldn't be able to concentrate on that job when he'd be thinking and worrying about Gisele. Besides, the New Orleans team would have left early that morning to be boots on the ground and ready when the client arrived with her entourage.

Rafael's hands curled into fists. He couldn't bail on this job. He had to be there for Gisele. She was his number one responsibility. Avoidance was not an option with her. He had to work through his own issues another time.

He ducked back into the bedroom and pulled on a T-shirt, jeans and boots. He checked the handgun he'd left lying on the nightstand.

Full magazine.

Check.

Safety on.

Check.

He pulled his shoulder holster out of the closet and laid it on the bed. When he went out today, he'd pack his weapon. One break-in might have been a crime of opportunity with strangers in town for the festival.

A second attempted break-in at the same building had been intentional. The intruder may or may not have been armed.

Rafael wasn't taking any chances. He'd be ready, and he'd be there for Gisele as a professional.

The personal stuff had to go on hold until Gisele was no longer threatened and he had the bandwidth to sort himself out.

Rafael squared his shoulders and emerged from the bedroom, determined to maintain focus no matter what.

Gisele met him with that beautiful smile that made his groin tighten and his thoughts scramble. "Ready?"

Oh, hell no.

He fought the urge to go back to the bedroom to wrangle his scattered brain cells before coming back out to face her. Instead, he gave her a brief nod and took a seat where she indicated at the tiny dinette.

She'd laid out their plates of eggs, cutlery, a small stack of toast and the jar of apple butter. "I warmed your coffee in the microwave. Be careful; it might be too hot."

"Thanks," he said, his voice gruff.

He picked up his fork and stared at the plate for a long moment.

A slim hand reached out and touched his thigh.

"Hey," Gisele spoke softly. "Whatever you're thinking...stop."

He looked up, his brow puckering.

"Just because I stayed last night doesn't mean I'll expect to stay forever. I'll be back in my own apartment tonight. Now, eat before your eggs get cold. I have a lot to do in the shop this morning."

He wanted to tell her he wasn't stewing over the fact she'd stayed the night. But that wouldn't have been true. Waking up with her in his apartment had changed everything.

And she believed she could fix it by going back to her place? That only made his gut knot tighter.

Fuck.

He stabbed his fork into his eggs.

He'd broken his own self-imposed rules. Now, he had to figure out where that left him.

As if totally unaware of the war being waged in Rafael's head, Gisele carried the burden of conversation. "We sold so much yesterday, I need to restock, and I'm also low on certain ingredients for my remedies. My grand-mère promised to bring what I need into town, but I have to meet her at the festival later this afternoon to get them." She ate her scrambled eggs and then selected a piece of toast from the stack, slathering a healthy portion of apple butter across the surface. "Today is the last day of the festival. It's usually the most hectic day and night with the biggest musical acts on stage. Things should calm down after the tourists leave tomorrow morning. We'll have a little residual surge through the shop, but then we'll be back to our normal seasonal traffic."

How could she sit across the table so cool, calm and beautiful when his insides were in panic mode?

She bit into her toast and chewed. "Will you be going to the boat factory today?"

He choked down the bite of egg he'd just taken and shook his head. "I'll be here all day."

She glanced around the apartment. "You don't have much left to unpack."

"I didn't have a lot to begin with. You don't accumulate a lot of things when you're always on the move."

She tilted her head and studied him. "You didn't have a house or apartment to come back to?"

"Sometimes. Then I'd get PCS orders and have to pack my shit and move or pay for a storage unit. It was easier to keep my physical assets to a minimum." He nodded toward the sofa and coffee table. "Besides the mattress in my bedroom, that's the first new furniture item I've purchased in ten years. I bought gently used stuff wherever I went and sold it when I shipped out."

Her hand paused with the piece of toast halfway to her mouth. "Not having a home had to be hard. You never married?" She bit into the toast without looking up.

The memory of him standing at the altar, waiting

patiently as the processional music started and stopped three times flashed through his mind. No one had come down the aisle. Not the flower girl or the ring bearer. Not the maid of honor or the bride's maids—until the bride's mother had stepped through the door and whispered into the ear of one of the male attendants. As the guy had hurried up a side aisle, Rafael could tell he wasn't happy. He'd passed Rafael and whispered in the preacher's ear.

The preacher had given Rafael an apologetic grimace and announced that the wedding would be postponed. The bride was indisposed.

Which translated to the bride had changed her mind and had run off in the limousine with the maid of honor.

For the first time since that day, Rafael didn't feel the hurt and anger of betrayal. At the time, he'd thought he was heartbroken. Now, he recognized the primary hurt he'd experienced was to his pride. He was lucky. He'd dodged a bullet that day. If he ever ran into his ex-fiancée, he'd thank her and wish her happiness with her wife.

So, in answer to Gisele's question, had he ever married...

"No," he said, without the usual anger that had cast a cloud over every relationship since his wedding. "I was stood up at the altar."

Gisele winced. "Ouch. I'm sorry."

"Don't be. It was for the best. I was more embarrassed than brokenhearted. I must not have really loved her. I was more in love with the idea of Love and marriage."

Gisele's eyes narrowed as she studied him. "Have you ever been really in love?" she asked so quietly he almost didn't make out her words.

The first thought that sprang to his mind and almost to his lips was *not until now.*

He clamped his lips tight. What was he thinking? In love?

He couldn't look away from the woman across from him. Her doe-brown eyes and shiny black hair, the smile that lit the room. Her patience with customers, her loyalty to her friends and family and her fierce independence all added up to a pretty amazing package.

Did he love her?

His pulse kicked up, and his palms grew clammy. She was still waiting for an answer to his question.

He could tell her to mind her own business or that he'd rather not say. When he opened his mouth, he simply said, "No."

No sooner had it left his lips than he knew it was a lie.

He'd watched Gisele for a while—before he'd pissed her off at the festival when she'd accused him of toying with her cousin's heart. He knew how the community loved her. It was part of the reason he had been intrigued by her.

He'd pursued her because she was always on his mind, unlike any other female he'd initially found attractive. He thought he could take her out a few times, get her out of his system, thoughts and mind and move on.

Boy, had he been wrong.

Gisele pushed back from the table, collected the plates and cutlery and carried them into the kitchenette.

Rafael followed. "I'll wash these," he said.

She responded with, "Then I'll dry."

They worked in silence for the next few minutes as they hand-washed the dishes, dried them and put them away. Working at her side felt as natural as breathing. All too soon, the task was done, and she went in search of her shoes.

Once she had them on, she looped her purse over her shoulder and headed for the door. "I hope you have a nice day," she said rather formally.

"Thank you," he responded, equally formally, as if they hadn't made love the night before or slept in each other's arms.

Gisele walked out of his apartment and down the stairs.

Rafael followed.

She stopped and faced him, her eyebrows dipping low on her forehead. "Where are you going?

"With you," he stated.

"No," she said, shaking her head. "It's daylight, I'm

going to my shop. Neither attack happened during the daylight hours."

"Both attacks were on your building," he reminded her. "They weren't crimes of opportunity. You were targeted."

"Still, no one will attack while others are around. I'll have a lot of people around me today. You don't need to be one of them."

He frowned. "I can't protect you if I'm not near you."

She gave him a tight smile. "Thank you for being so conscientious, but I don't need protection while I'm working today." She turned and walked away.

Not to be deterred, Rafael followed her. "At least let me clear the building before you go in."

"We would've heard if anyone tried to get in," she said as she stuck her key in the lock.

"Not if he figured out how to disarm the alarms."

"Is that possible without getting inside first?"

"No," Rafael said.

"Thought so." She pushed open the door and stepped inside.

Rafael eased past her before she could close the door between them. He grinned. "I promise, you won't even know I'm here."

Gisele rolled her eyes. "Right. I won't know there's a bull in my China shop." She sighed. "Fine. You can stay, but try not to get in the way."

"Let me help you restock shelves. You'll find I'm trainable. I got high marks in my obedience class."

"You're too much," she said and put him to work loading items on the Voodoo doll rack.

He shook his head as he hung the dolls, amazed that so many people purchased them. He would feel sorry for the people they targeted with the pins if he believed they really worked. Like so many things unique to Louisiana, it was the novelty of the item more than the use.

Gisele's assistant, Lena, arrived and went to work sweeping and mopping the floors. The shop wouldn't open for another hour.

Before Lena's mopping could box him into a corner, Gisele appeared, carrying a bucket of soapy water, a squeegee and a dry shop rag. "You can clean the outside windows while the floor is drying."

"Keep the back door locked," he warned.

"I will. I leaned the ladder against the back wall. You'll need it." She shooed him out the door, leaving it unlocked, but the sign on the door remained CLOSED.

Rafael set the bucket, squeegee and rag on the stoop and hurried around back to collect the ladder. Once he had it set up in front of the building, he went to work washing the windows, taking pleasure in a purely physical task where he could see the fruits of his labors in the finished job.

He had the work done before the store opened. In

the process of cleaning windows, he noticed areas of the exterior that needed minor maintenance. He nailed down loose siding, caulked around the clean windows and tightened the screws holding the striped awning over the front. When he'd finished outside, he carried the ladder to the rear and stowed it in the stock room.

After the store opened, he worked inside, careful to stay as far out of the way as possible in the tight confines between rows of goods and display racks. When the shop became too crowded, he moved into the back of the store and cleaned the shelves in a storage room, the toilet and replaced the filters in the air vents.

Close to the end of the day, the crowd thinned for a few minutes. Gisele let Lena leave early to catch the band playing that night at the festival.

Rafael stepped up beside Gisele.

She moved money from the cash drawer to the safe below, closed the safe and spun the lock. She straightened in time to smile and welcome a customer who'd just entered the shop.

"How do you do it?" he asked.

Her brow wrinkled as she shifted items on the counter. "Do what?"

"Keep smiling after a long day on your feet."

She shrugged. "I remind myself that I work for myself, not a bloodless financial firm that doesn't give two rat's asses about the people they represent."

She smiled up at him. “I can go to bed at night with a clear conscience.”

He brushed his hand across her cheek. “You’re a good person, Gisele.”

“I try.” She glanced past him. “Excuse me. That customer looks like he has a question.” Gisele moved around him and approached the customer.

The man had shaggy dark hair and a stubbled face that looked like it hadn’t seen a razor in a few days. He stared around the store with a frown as if looking for something but not finding it. His hands were stuffed into the pockets of a lightweight jacket.

Who wore a jacket, even a lightweight one, in south Louisiana during the summer? He wasn’t like the hordes of other customers who’d been through that day. This man had entered alone.

Rafael followed Gisele and pretended to rearrange items on a shelf close by, keeping the man in view through his peripheral vision and in range should he try anything.

CHAPTER 12

GISELE APPROACHED the customer with a smile on her face. "Can I help you?"

He turned to her, his brow wrinkled. "I was in this store a few years ago. Wasn't it a pawn shop or an antique store?"

"Yes, sir," Gisele said. "It was an antique store before I purchased it a little over three years ago."

He nodded. "I thought so. It had some interesting antiques in it. I haven't had a chance to get back here until now and hoped some of the items would still be available. How long have you worked here?"

"I purchased the property a little over three years ago," Gisele said.

"Do you know where I can contact the former owner? The antique dealer?"

"I'm sorry," Gisele said. "I was told he died of a stroke."

"Do you know what happened to all the antiques?"

"As a matter of fact, I do," she said. "His family sold the store to me as is, with everything in it. They didn't want to deal with trying to dispose of or sell what was left. I hired an auction company to come in and sell the contents."

The man's face pinched. "Oh, that's too bad. There was one piece in particular I was interested in. A vintage brass cash register mounted on a wood cabinet. You wouldn't happen to know where it ended up, would you?"

Gisele smiled. "Actually, I know the piece you're talking about. It was a beautiful piece in great condition. I kept it, thinking I might use it when I remodeled and made this a gift shop. But I needed something more modern, and the vintage one took up a lot of floor space."

The front door opened. A gaggle of girls entered. They giggled and pointed at different items on display racks and shelves.

One of them looked toward Gisele and waved a hand. "Excuse me. Could you help us?"

Gisele turned toward the girls. "I'll be right there." When she started to walk away, the man laid a hand on her arm.

"What did you do with the old register? Is it still here in the store?" he asked eagerly.

Rafael stepped up beside Gisele and stared down at the shorter man. "Need any help, sweetheart?"

She pulled her arm free of the man's grasp. "I don't think so," she gave the stranger a tight smile and added, "do I?"

The man looked from Gisele to Rafael and moved back a step. "No, ma'am. Just curious what happened to the old register."

"I gave it away," she said and walked away with Rafael.

After dealing with the giggling girls, she looked around for the strange man with a thing for vintage cash registers.

"He left," Rafael said from his position near Johnny's cage.

"Good." Gisele crossed to the counter, locked the register, slung her purse over her shoulder and dug out her key. "I need to feed Johnny, lock up and get to the festival before seven." She hurried to the front door before any more customers wandered in.

"Why the festival?" Rafael asked, following her.

"Madame Gautier is holding court," she said with a twisted smile.

"The Voodoo queen?" Rafael asked. "Your grand-mère?"

"Yes, sir." She stepped through and waited for Rafael to follow. Once he was outside, she locked the door, hurried around the side of the building and climbed the stairs to her apartment.

When he followed, she didn't bother to argue. Once she unlocked her door, she stood to the side and let Rafael enter first.

He performed his sweep and waved her inside.

She headed straight for her bedroom, dropping her purse on the sofa as she passed. "Could you get the remaining half of the mango out of the refrigerator and tear off a leaf from the head of lettuce? I'd like to get a quick shower and change out of the clothes I've worn now for two days straight."

"Go," he said. "I'll get Johnny's beer."

Gisele peeled off the shirt and skirt as she hurried through the bedroom. She dropped them in the laundry basket along with her bra and panties. Standing naked in her bedroom, heat surged through her, heading south to her core, tempting her to ask Rafael if he wanted to join her in the shower.

After a quick glance at the clock, she ruled that out. Her grand-mère would only stay at the festival until seven o'clock. That didn't give her much time. She needed the ingredients she'd asked her to bring. Even more, she needed her grand-mère's advice.

She didn't wait for the water to warm before she stepped into the shower. The cool spray tamped down the fire burning inside. She quickly washed her hair and body, her hand going to her sex, deliciously sore from making love to Rafael. And just like that, she was on fire again.

She rinsed, stepped out of the shower and dried

quickly. After yanking a brush through her hair, she left it down to air-dry. She threw on a sapphire blue peasant blouse that draped off her shoulders. To complement the rich color of the top, she slipped into a long, flowing skirt in a variety of colors that would make a peacock proud.

Gifted with naturally long, thick black eyelashes and light brown skin, she didn't need much in the way of makeup. A touch of lipstick and a pair of sandals, and she was done in less than ten minutes.

When Gisele emerged from her bedroom, Rafael let out a long, low whistle. "Wow."

Heat rushed up her neck and into her cheeks. "Thanks. Grand-mère Gautier likes it when I represent the family heritage in something...colorful."

"Should I change into something more formal?" he asked.

Her gaze swept over him from head to toe, drinking in his fine details. The man would look good in a tuxedo or a gunny sack. With his coal-black hair and brown-black eyes, the black polo shirt and black jeans he wore made him look a little dark and dangerous. "No. You look good in what you have on."

He held up the mango and lettuce as she'd requested. "Then let's get Johnny his beer, woman." His eyes twinkled, making Gisele flush with heat and pleasure. She could get used to having him around.

Don't go there, she warned herself. It would only cause her heartache.

They locked her apartment and returned to the shop to the sound of Johnny calling out, *Get me a beer, woman.*

Rafael chuckled and headed straight for Johnny's cage.

Gisele walked to the back of the shop to the storage room where she retrieved a scoop of bird seed. When she came out, she found Rafael with his hand in Johnny's cage, feeding him the mango. He laid the fruit on the floor.

She shook her head, "Are you sure you don't have Cajun magic in your blood?"

"Not that I know of."

"Here, you can put the feed in his dish." She handed him the scoop and watched as Johnny stood by and let him fill the bowl.

As Rafael pulled his hand out of the cage, Johnny flapped his wings.

Cheeky bastard.

"I really need to work on his vocabulary," Gisele said.

"I don't know," Rafael secured the door and paused to study the parrot. "It's colorful like him. I kind of like his phrases."

Johnny spread his wings as if showing off his flamboyant plumage as he squawked, *He's a keeper.*

"That's right." Rafael glanced at Gisele. "You heard the bird. He tells it like it is."

Gisele smiled. If only he would allow himself to be a keeper.

Johnny was on a roll. *You break it, you buy it, asshole.*

This phrase struck closer to home. If she allowed her heart to be broken, she owned it. She'd have no one to blame but herself.

She really needed to talk with her grand-mère. Maybe she could steer her in the right direction in matters of the heart.

"It's getting late," Gisele said. "I need to get to the festival before she leaves." *And before I do something really stupid like fall for this guy.*

"Later, Johnny," Rafael said to the bird.

Johnny flapped and called out after them, *Cheeky bastard.*

"I think he likes you," Gisele said as she locked the front door.

"Because he doesn't bite me?" Rafael asked.

"That, and he keeps calling you cheeky bastard," Gisele smiled.

"Doesn't he call everyone that?"

"Not as often as he does with you. I think it's his love language."

He grinned and slipped an arm around her waist. "Like yours is chocolate éclairs?"

She smiled and leaned into him. "Every time." When Rafael was like this, all playful and sweet, she could forget that he'd warned her he wasn't into commitment and that, one day soon, he'd move on.

Well, hell. What was the saying?

It was better to have loved and lost than never to have loved at all.

As long as she knew what she was letting herself get into, what would it hurt?

Her heart.

Her NYC douchebag ex-boyfriend had hurt her pride and pissed her off. Losing him hadn't touched her heart.

How would she feel if she let herself love Rafael and he walked away?

As if someone had kicked her in the gut, ripped her heart out and left her broken and bleeding in a ditch.

She really needed advice.

Her friends had warned her not to get involved.

Maybe her grand-mère would have something better to say…like, *go with your heart, even if you know it'll break.*

Rafael led her to his truck parked behind his apartment and handed her up into the passenger seat.

She settled in and buckled her seatbelt.

Rafael climbed into the driver's seat and drove the short distance to the edge of town where the festival was taking place. He entered the field roped off for parking and followed the ground guides to where they wanted him to stop. He parked, got out and hurried around to help Gisele down.

Though she loved her independence, she also loved that he cared enough to make sure she was safe. It might be his job as a Brotherhood Protector, but he did it with the utmost respect and grace.

Once she was on the ground, he reached for her hand and held it as they entered the festival grounds.

"Where will we find the infamous Madam Gautier?" he asked, craning his neck as she searched the array of tents.

"About that..." Gisele squeezed his hand. "She really knows her Voodoo, natural remedies and magic and helps people every way she can. But during the Zydeco Festival, she reads palms and donates the money to the women's shelter."

Gisele brought Rafael to a halt in front of a tent made of dark purple velvet with a fanciful sign proclaiming Madam Gautier—Palm Reader and Fortune Teller.

Rafael grinned. "I love it. And it's for a good cause."

Gisele sighed. "I want you to meet the woman who raised me. My grand-mère." She leaned close to the tent door and called out softly. "Are you in there and alone?"

A voice with a heavy Cajun accent answered in a tone meant to give the listener chills. "Enter only if you dare. See into da future. Oui, Gisele, I'm in here and alone. What took you so long?"

With her hand on the velvet curtain hanging over the door, she lifted her chin and spoke a little louder, giving an introduction worthy of her grand-mère. "Enter the realm of the amazing, the myth, the legend, Bayou Mambaloa's own Voodoo Queen, Madam Gautier." She flung back the curtain and waved Rafael through with a flourish.

He ducked his head and stepped into the small tent big enough really for only the fortune teller and one customer.

Gisele squeezed in behind Rafael.

"Sit!" Madam Gautier commanded.

When Rafael moved to let Gisele sit in the only chair positioned directly across from her, grand-mère, Madam Gautier, glared. "No, no, no!" She pointed a gnarled finger at Rafael. "You will sit."

Rafael shot a glance toward Gisele.

She nodded.

"You need not permission when Madam Gautier commands." She waved her hand.

Rafael dropped into the seat.

"Your hand," she demanded. "Give me your hand."

He held out his hand as if he would shake hers. "Rafael Romero, it's a pleasure to meet you."

"Yeah, yeah, yeah. Always a pleasure." Instead of shaking his hand, she yanked it toward her, positioning it beneath the light hanging over the table. She turned it palm upward and stared at the lines.

Any other person would have laughed at the woman's crazed expression and intensity.

Not Gisele. She'd learned long ago that her grand-mère was special. Magical. She couldn't explain how her grand-mère knew the things she knew or conjured spells and potions much more complicated than what Gisele experimented with. She just knew to trust that what she did was real.

Rafael had the decency not to laugh. He gave the woman his hand and his attention.

"You have faced danger and survived. Not once, but many times."

Rafael nodded.

"Love has eluded you when you in da past, giving you da chance to mature and know what you truly want and to allow you to recognize when it comes to you." She leaned closer, her eyes narrowing, a crease forming across her forehead. "You will face another challenge dat will test your beliefs, test your strength and heart and da depth of your commitment. Do not hesitate, or you will lose all."

She shoved his hand back across the table and leaned her head back. Drawing in a deep breath, she let it out slowly. She inhaled again and let out quickly, her head coming down, her gaze meeting Rafael's. "You are sleeping with my granddaughter?"

Rafael leaned back, his eyes wide. "Madam?"

She waved her hand, dismissing his questioning glance. "Of course you are." She flung her hand toward the curtained door. "Leave. I wish to speak with Gisele."

Rafael rose to his feet, his gaze going to Gisele.

"It's okay. I'll only be a few minutes," she said and stepped aside so he could exit.

Once Rafael was outside the tent and the curtain dropped, Gisele sank into the chair he'd vacated, the warmth of his body seeping into hers.

"You came for da ingredients?" her grand-mère asked.

"Yes, grand-mère," she responded.

Madam Gautier reached beneath the table, pulled out a canvas tote and handed it across the table. "I will see you Sunday night for dinner?"

Gisele nodded. "Yes, grand-mère."

The older woman lifted her chin toward the door. "Bring your man."

Gisele shook her head and lowered her voice to a whisper. "He's not my man. That's what I wanted to talk to you about. I need your advice."

"Give me your hand," her grand-mère demanded.

Gisele complied, laying her hand in her grand-mère's. "I don't want a palm reading. I want to know what to do. I think I'm in love with him. I've only known him for a couple of days. It's happened so fast. Can what I'm feeling be real?"

"Shh. Stop talking." Her grand-mère stared at her

palm, studying it for a long time before speaking. "Like your man, you have faced hardships and survived, becoming stronger and more certain of your course. You give so much to others yet hesitate to take what you want and need. Soon, a challenge will present itself."

Her grand-mère's hand tightened around hers. "A life-and-death challenge. If you successfully over-come the challenge, you will know da path to take to find love. You must believe in yourself and believe in da magic of love." The older woman raised a hand to cup Gisele's cheek. "My Gisele, you're beautiful, inside and out. I've always loved you. Never lose sight of your worth and draw on your strength within."

Gisele laid her hand over her grand-mère's and leaned into it, pressing a kiss to the older woman's palm. "And I love you."

"Now, go," her grand-mère said. "Your man is waiting."

Gisele wanted her grand-mère to give her advice as her grand-mère. She needed to know what to do in plain language she could easily understand. Instead, she got the fortuneteller version in shadowy vagueness that rarely revealed its meaning until it slapped one in the face.

Having grown up with her grand-mère, she knew when she'd been dismissed. No amount of pleading would net her the straightforward guidance she so desperately craved. She wanted to make the right decision about Rafael.

But what was it? And what did her grand-mère's message mean? She'd sat in on numerous readings in the past with her grand-mère. What she'd just witnessed wasn't like the advice she'd given to any of the others. There was no discussion about the lines crisscrossing her palm, what each individual one represented and how it pertained to her particular path in life.

What life-or-death challenge would she face? Did it have to do with the break-ins? Would she recognize it in time to save herself or the ones she loved?

She slowly stood and turned toward the exit.

"Gisele," her grand-mère said softly.

She turned, hoping her grand-mère would have more definitive words.

Her grand-mère nodded toward the table. "Don't forget your bag."

Gisele almost laughed. Well, the words had been more definitive than the palm reading. She took the bag and left the tent.

Rafael stood right outside the door, his gaze meeting hers. "Are you okay?"

Gisele nodded.

Rafael held out his hand.

She slipped hers into his.

They walked away from the tent, each lost in their own thoughts.

"Gisele!" a voice called out several times before Gisele realized it was her name. She turned to find YaYa hurrying toward her.

"Hey, YaYa." Gisele pulled her hand free of Rafael's. "What's up?"

"Did those men find you?"

Gisele frowned. "What men?"

YaYa's brow creased. "I stopped to drop off supplies at the studio. Two men were standing outside your shop. I told them you closed at five, and that you'd be open again tomorrow 'round ten."

"Did they say what they wanted?" Rafael asked.

"They asked who owned the building. They might be interested in purchasing it. They sent one of their brokers ahead to scout and hadn't heard from him. They were worried about him and came to see if anyone had seen him."

Gisele shook her head. "No one's contacted me about purchasing my shop. It's not for sale."

YaYa nodded. "I told them you probably wouldn't be interested. They still wanted to find their agent."

"Did they give you a name or description of the guy?" Rafael asked.

"They did." YaYa squinted. "Ronald something… Roland Caney. One of the men described him as short and about so high." The yoga studio owner held her hand several inches over Gisele's head. "Dark, shaggy hair. Might have been wearing a gray jacket.

Which is crazy in this heat." She shook her head. "Ring any bells?"

"You say they were interested in my building?" Gisele asked.

YaYa nodded. "That's what they said."

"Gisele!" Another feminine voice called out, drawing Gisele's attention from YaYa.

She turned to find Amelia Aubert heading their way. "Oh, I'm glad I caught you. Did those men find you?"

"What men?" Gisele asked.

"Two big guys came into the bakery this afternoon right before I closed and asked if I knew who owned the Mamba Wamba Gift Shop." She glanced at YaYa. "Hey, YaYa. Heard you had a record enrollment for your early morning yoga session. My sales increased as well. Your clients meet at the bakery after your session."

Gisele frowned. "What guys, and what did you tell them?"

Amelia turned back to Gisele. "Sorry. Two big guys. They said they were with the state Historical Society and wanted to ask questions about your building. They said they sent a representative ahead but hadn't heard from him, so they came themselves to check it out."

"Did they tell you his name?" Gisele asked.

"Yes, they did," Amelia said.

YaYa crossed her arms over her chest. "Would it happen to be Roland Caney?"

Amelia's eyes widened. "As a matter of fact, it was." Her eyebrows descended. "You know him?"

"No," YaYa said. "I think those same two guys showed up in front of the Mamba Wamba a little while ago, saying they were interested in purchasing Gisele's place and that they'd sent a broker ahead but hadn't heard back from him." She paused and gave Amelia a pointed look. "They were looking for Roland Caney."

Amelia's eyebrows rose up her forehead. "But my guys said they were from the historical society. Come to think of it, they didn't look like they were all that interested in history."

"More like bouncers at a strip club," YaYa said.

"Yeah," Amelia said, nodding.

"Gisele!" another feminine voice called out behind Gisele.

YaYa laughed. "Aren't you the popular one tonight?"

The three women and Rafael turned to find Deputy Shelby Taylor headed their way in her maternity uniform.

"What are you doing working so late?" Gisele asked as Shelby came to stand in front of her.

"I'm filling in for one of the deputies who was supposed to assist with the festival. His kid fell out of a tree this afternoon and broke his arm. He's getting it set now. Anyway, I wanted to tell you something interesting I learned today at the sheriff's office about that guy we saw at the Crawdad Hole last night."

Gisele shook her head. Was she living in an alternate universe or a really weird dream? "The guy in the light gray jacket with the dark, shaggy hair?"

Amelia and YaYa's eyes widened.

"Yeah, that guy," Shelby looked from Gisele to YaYa and Amelia, her brow furrowing. "Something about his face seemed familiar. When I went to work this morning, I realized why." She pulled a sheet of paper from her pocket and unfolded it. On it was the mug shot of a man with shaggy dark hair and stubble on his face. His mug shot indicated he was five feet seven inches. The name on the mug shot was...

Gisele turned to Rafael. "Roland Caney. The guy who came into the shop this afternoon asking about antiques."

"He came into your shop?" Shelby asked.

"Yeah." A creepy feeling of déjà vu slithered across the back of Gisele's neck, making the hairs stand up. She moved closer to Rafael and slipped her hand into his. "He said he'd been in the building a few years back when it was an antique store."

"It would have to have been a few years ago," Shelby said. "He was in jail for the past three and a half years for robbing a convenience store. He made parole three days ago and immediately ghosted his parole officer. Thus, the picture that floated through with a BOLO alert."

"BOLO?" Amelia asked.

"Be on the lookout," Shelby said. "And he was in your shop, looking for antiques?" She shook her head. "That doesn't make sense. You'd think he'd be laying low to keep from getting caught and sent straight back to jail."

"Why would he ask about antiques if he was on the run?" Gisele shook her head. "You're right. It doesn't make sense."

"If you see him, call 911. He got out on good behavior and a few pulled strings, but he was convicted of assault with a deadly weapon." Shelby held Gisele's gaze. "Consider him dangerous."

Gisele's gut clenched.

Shelby turned to Rafael. "I wasn't too keen on you hanging out with our girl, Gisele, given your reputation with women."

Rafael nodded. "I get that."

Shelby's lips pressed together in a formidable line for a pregnant woman. "But I'm willing to grant you grace as long as you keep her safe until this Caney dude is back behind bars."

"What about the other two guys?" YaYa asked.

Shelby frowned. "What other two guys?"

YaYa filled the deputy on hers and Amelia's

encounter with the men interested in the Mamba Wamba building and the missing Roland Caney.

Shelby got on her radio and reported the two suspicious men also looking for Caney. When she'd completed the call, she turned back to Gisele. "I'm worried about you."

Gisele snorted softly. "Frankly, I'm a little worried about myself, as well."

"You can't stay at your apartment while Caney is at large," Shelby said. "If you want, you can come stay with me."

Gisele shook her head. "If I'm in any kind of danger, and someone comes looking for me, that danger could impact whoever I'm with. Thanks, Shelby, but no. I'd never forgive myself if something happened to you or your baby."

"You could stay with me," YaYa said. "Lord knows, I'm not pregnant. I'm not a candidate for immaculate conception. It's been a long time since I got laid."

"You could stay with me," Amelia said. "I'm not pregnant and don't have kids."

Rafael squeezed Gisele's hand gently. "She's staying with me."

Gisele drew in a deep breath and let it out slowly.

Rafael glanced down at her and amended, "If that's all right with you."

She'd conducted a conversation with a man who'd been convicted of aggravated assault. Not only was it all right that Rafael insisted she stay with him, but being with the Navy SEAL was the *only* place she felt marginally safe.

She met his gaze and nodded. "Yes, please."

CHAPTER 13

RAFAEL HUSTLED Gisele out to the parking area, remaining hyper-aware of everything around them. He'd had a bad feeling about the man in her store that afternoon and could kick himself for not standing between them instead of to the side.

Had he been armed, Caney could have hurt Gisele before Rafael could have stopped him.

Once Gisele was safely buckled in the passenger seat, Rafael climbed into the driver's seat, pulled out his cell phone and started to call Remy. Before Rafael hit send, he remembered his regional lead was on a project in New Orleans, as was most of the team.

He scrolled through his favorites, hit the number for Hank Patterson and put the call on speaker.

The founder of the Brotherhood Protectors answered on the first ring. "Romero. What's happening?"

"Got you on speaker with Ms. Gautier in the vehicle with me."

"Ms. Gautier, Hank Patterson. I hear you had a break-in."

"Yes, sir," she said. "We're up to two attempts now."

"Okay, then," Hank said. "I'm glad Romero insisted on sticking around as your protector. Any leads on the intruder?"

"We have a name we need your guy Swede to check into," Rafael said.

"Hang on," Hank said. "Let me get him online."

A moment later, Hank was back. "Got Swede on with Romero and his client, Ms. Gautier. Talk."

"I need you to find out anything you can about a Roland Caney," Rafael said. "He's an ex-con, convicted of robbery and aggravated assault, spent time in jail, recently released on parole and already skipped out on his parole officer."

"Sounds like you've got the scoop on him. Are you looking for anything in particular?" Swede asked with a clicking sound in the background. The computer guru would already have the name entered in a search engine as he spoke.

"He showed up today at Ms. Gautier's shop," Rafael said. "He was asking about antiques that used to be in the store before Ms. Gautier purchased and renovated the building three years ago."

"Ballsy of him to show up in public when he's violated his parole," Hank said.

"Exactly," Rafael said. "Anything you can find on him might help us understand why he's targeting Gisele—Ms. Gautier and her store."

Gisele leaned over the console and whispered, "Tell him about the two guys."

Rafael nodded. "Also, two guys showed up in town asking about Ms. Gautier and her place. They are looking for Caney, claiming they sent him as either an agent of the Historical Society or a real estate broker. The ladies who spoke to the men described them as big and tough-looking like bouncers at a strip club."

"Got any names on them?" Swede asked.

"No."

"Would there be any video surveillance footage available in the area that might have captured them?"

"The auto parts store next to the bakery might have picked up the two guys," Gisele said.

"I'll look into it," Swede said.

"Anything else?" Hank asked.

Rafael glanced at Gisele.

She shrugged.

"No, sir," Rafael said.

"Let us know of any changes in the situation," Hank said.

"Roger," Rafael responded. "Out here." He ended the call and turned to Gisele. "Are you okay?"

She nodded. “A little unnerved, but okay.”

Rafael pulled out of the parking area and onto the road leading into town.

“I don’t understand why a man who violated his parole would show up in Bayou Mambaloa, asking about antiques from a store sold over three years ago.” Gisele shook her head. “Retail stores change hands, especially if it has been a number of years since you last went there.”

“Perhaps the same number of years Caney spent in jail…?” Rafael shot a glance toward Gisele.

“That would track.” Gisele’s brow furrowed. “He was asking about one item in particular. A vintage brass cash register. If Caney was the intruder both times, and he asked specifically about the brass cash register, do you think he was trying to get in to find it?”

“You told him you gave it away,” Rafael glanced her way.

“He seemed very interested in where he might find it.” Gisele’s frown deepened, and her face paled. “I didn’t tell him who I gave it to,” she looked across the cab at Rafael, “did I?”

“No.” Rafael returned his attention to the road ahead. “You went to help that group of girls that came in. He left while you were working with them. Why?”

“I gave that register to Grand-mère,” she said.

“Any idea what it was worth?” Rafael asked.

She nodded. "It was brass and came fully installed in a solid oak cabinet with drawers. It was in excellent shape. The unit was valued at anywhere between five and ten thousand dollars."

"That's a substantial amount of money," Rafael said, "but it's not an easy item to transport and even harder to sell. Does anyone else know who you gave that register to?"

Gisele shrugged. "I didn't make a big deal about it. Everything else was auctioned off. I had the auctioneer transport the register to Grand-mère's house and place it in her sitting room. It's an odd piece for a house but strangely fits in with her eclectic style."

Rafael's cell phone rang. He fished it out of his pocket and glanced down at the caller ID.

Swede.

He answered the call. "Romero here. Going on speaker."

"Got something on Caney. Not sure if it relates to what's going on with Ms. Gautier's store. Caney won big at the horse races. Two hundred and fifty thousand dollars on a long shot named Lucky Seven. He cashed in and disappeared. Three days later, he was arrested for aggravated assault at a convenience store. He had no money on him except for the amount he stole from the till at the convenience store."

"Did they find the two hundred fifty thousand dollars he'd won at the horse race?" Rafael asked.

"No. Sources on the dark web reported Caney as upside down in gambling debt." Swede said. "He owed the New Orleans Mafia more than that, and it was compounding daily."

"They would've wanted him to use that money to pay down or off that debt," Rafael surmised.

"With that in mind, I got into the security surveillance database serving the auto parts store next door to the Bayou Bakery. I found the two big guys who asked about Mama Wamba, Ms. Gautier and Roland Caney. I ran their facial images through an online database search. Bingo. The two guys are members of the New Orleans mafia."

"Now it all makes sense," Gisele said. "With the mafia on his heels, Caney hid the money somewhere, intending to get back to it after he lost his tail."

Rafael nodded. "And it took him all this time to come back for it because he stashed all of it and didn't save out any to live on."

"So, he robbed a convenience store, got caught and was sent to jail," Swede concluded. "That's all I've got for now. Let me know if you need anything else. Out here." Swede ended the call.

Gisele reached out and touched Rafael's arm. "Turn around."

He slowed at the urgency in her voice. "Where are we going now?"

"I'm betting it's somewhere in the cash register cabinet."

"The one you gave to your grandmother?"

"Yes. Head south out of the opposite end of town," she said. "We need to find that money before Caney and before the goons from the New Orleans mafia catch wind of its location."

Rafael drove through town and took the road leaning south.

Gisele pulled her cell phone out of her purse and called her grand-mère. It rang four times and went to voice mail.

"Grand-mère, this is Gisele. I'm headed over to your place. Don't go anywhere until we get there." She ended the call and sat with her phone in her lap, her gaze on the road ahead. "I don't like that she didn't answer her phone."

"Does she always answer her phone when you call?" Rafael asked.

"Not always. Her house is outside of town, perched on the edge of the bayou. Cell phone service can be sketchy at best." She shook her head. "You don't think they figured out where the cash register is, do you?"

"I doubt it. That was a few years back. People forget, especially if it doesn't pertain to them directly."

"Grand-mère should be there before us. She was scheduled to leave the festival right after we saw her."

Gisele leaned forward, her face tense. "After the next curve, slow down and look for a gravel road on the right."

He eased into the curve and slowed coming out of it.

"There." Gisele pointed to a narrow, one-lane gravel road.

He left the highway and drove the length of the gravel road beneath a canopy of interwoven limbs of the giant oak trees lining the drive. The road opened onto a sweeping lawn surrounding a two-story colonial with wraparound porches on both levels.

Rafael didn't voice it, but the house wasn't what he expected of a Voodoo Queen.

Gisele chuckled. "Not what you expected? Too often, people stereotype Voodoo practitioners as flamboyant and over the top with makeup and facial tattoos." She grimaced. "Flamboyant like the grand-mère you saw this evening. That was all for show to play to what the audience expects. She works in her kitchen wearing leggings and oversized T-shirts, looking like an aging college coed." She smiled softly and looked around. "Her car is here. Come on. Let's get inside and warn her about what might be headed her way."

Rafael slid from his seat onto the ground and hurried around to help Gisele alight. "The sooner we locate the money, the sooner we can get it away from here."

"If it's even here." Gisele leaned up on her toes to press her lips to his. "Thank you for insisting on staying in Bayou Mambaloa to protect me."

He pulled her into his arms and kissed her hard. "I couldn't walk away and leave you."

"You could have had one of your other team members babysit me," she said.

Rafael thought of Valentin and Landry staying with Gisele and shook his head. "No."

She grinned. "Look at you committing to more than a day or two with one woman. You're making progress."

A frown settled across Rafael's forehead.

Gisele touched his arm. "I'm just kidding. This is different. I'm a client. Once the threat is gone, I'll be gone."

His frown didn't lighten. He didn't want to think about what would happen after Gisele's threat was neutralized. He'd move on to the next project or bodyguard assignment. She'd go back to her gift shop. They'd pass often since he lived next door to her. Maybe they'd become friends.

The problem was, he couldn't see her as just a friend. He'd made love to her, experienced the magic of her passion and the beauty of her spirit. Walking away from all that she was would be harder than he could imagine.

She reached for his hand. "Come on, let's find the stash."

They walked up the steps to the wide wooden porch. Rafael knocked on the front door.

"Grand-mère!" Gisele called out.

Silence.

She peered through a window. "Her car is here, but I don't see anyone moving inside."

Gisele walked around the side of the house.

Rafael followed.

She paused at the back corner, staring out at the bayou and the dock, bathed in silvery moonlight. The dock was empty. Her grand-mère's pirogue wasn't where it was usually tied. "She's out on the bayou. Let's go inside. I have a key to her house." She led the way to the front door.

She pulled her keychain out of her purse, thumbed through the various keys and selected one. Moments later, the door was open, and they entered the house.

Gisele led Rafael straight into a room with an odd collection of antique furniture and modern art. On the far side, tucked into a corner, stood the brass cash resister perched atop a wooden cabinet, pushed up against the wall.

They hurried across the room and stopped in front of the antique.

Rafael hit the button that made the cash drawer pop out. It was empty except for an old bobby pin and a paper clip. He felt around the drawer and tugged on the dividers, looking for secret panels hidden beneath. When the cash drawer didn't yield answers, Gisele worked her way down the front of the cabinet.

One by one, she pulled the drawers all the way out, inspected the slots and then slit them back in. When she reached the bottom drawer, she tried to open it, but it was stuck. No matter how hard she pulled, it wouldn't open.

"Let me try." Rafael worked on it for a few minutes and frowned. "We might need tools to dislodge that drawer."

"Grand-mère keeps tools in the storage room beneath the servants' staircase at the back of the house. What do we need?"

"I'll find something that will work." He hurried to the back of the house, where he located the storage room with built-in cabinets and a huge metal toolbox loaded with a variety of tools. He didn't take long to find a hammer, chisel and crowbar.

As he hurried back across the house, he heard voices. His heartbeat slammed to a stop, then raced ahead. He slipped into the shadows and listened.

The soft murmur was Gisele. The other was decidedly male.

Rafael checked his cell phone.

No service. He couldn't even call for backup.

Squaring his shoulders, he inched forward, carefully placing his feet to avoid squeaky floorboards.

As he neared the room where he'd left Gisele, he

paused behind a potted Ficus tree. From where he stood, he could make out what the man was saying and see into the room.

The man with the shaggy hair and gray jacket held a gun pointed at Gisele.

Caney.

"Of course, the drawer won't open," he said with a sneer in his tone. "I glued it shut to keep the contents safe until I could return."

Holding a gun in front of him, he tried to move the drawer with his free hand. "I guess it's a good thing it's stuck. It kept people out all these years." He rocked the top-heavy unit until it teetered precariously. With a final shove, the register fell, crashing to the floor, making the entire house shudder.

The brass register took the brunt of the fall, bashing into a nearby antique end table, shattering it. The wooden cabinet remained intact.

"You're not going to make this easy, are you?" Caney grumbled. He raised his foot and stomped the cabinet.

Nothing broke free.

He stomped again.

All the while Caney stomped, Gisele's gaze remained on the doorway into the hall.

Rafael tensed and bunched his muscles, preparing to rush into the room and overpower Caney before he could harm Gisele.

As he straightened, the front door slammed open, and two bulldozer-sized men clomped in.

Rafael shrank back into the leaves of the Ficus tree.

Bulldozer One called out in a thundering voice, "Caney!"

Caney muttered a curse from within the room containing the cash register.

The two mafia thugs made their way down the hall, carrying handguns at the ready and looking into room after room on either side until they found their guy, Caney.

"Gentleman," Caney said. "You're just in time."

Bulldozer One pointed his gun at Caney. "The boss wants his money. Yesterday."

"I was in the process of getting it." Caney pointed his pistol at the cabinet lying on its side. "It's in that."

"Then get it out," the bulldozer demanded.

"Apparently, they built furniture to last in the early nineteen hundreds." Caney raised his eyebrows. "Happen to have a sledgehammer?"

Bulldozer One's eyes narrowed.

Caney continued, "No? Then I'll need to find one and break the wood. No one's getting anything out of it until then."

The more talkative man of the two tanks motioned for the other one to walk up to the cabinet.

One mighty stomp from the heavier-set guy and the base of the wooden cabinet splintered. A second effectively placed stomp broke the cabinet into pieces.

Caney dropped to his hands and knees and sifted through the splintered wood. The longer he searched, the more frantic his movements became.

"The money," Chatty mafia guy pressed.

"It was in the bottom drawer." Caney sat back on his heels, shoved a hand through his hair and stared at the damaged cabinet. "I sealed it. No one should've been able to get into it." He looked at the men. "You have to believe me."

"Tell it to the boss." Bulldozer One motioned with his gun. "Let's go."

His partner pointed his gun at Gisele, standing quietly in the corner. "What about her? Maybe she knows where the money is."

All three pairs of eyes shifted to Gisele.

She held up her hands. "I don't know what you're talking about."

"The money that was in this cabinet," Caney said. "There was two-hundred and fifty thousand dollars in that bottom drawer. What did you do with it?" He lurched to his feet, his eyes wide and slightly crazed. "I waited over three years to come back and get my money. Where did you put it, bitch?"

Caney backhanded Gisele so hard she staggered backward. He grabbed her by her hair and yanked her back to him, shoving the gun against her temple. "Where's the damn money?"

Rage exploded inside Rafael. He flung himself out from behind the tree. Never mind he was outnumbered, three guns to one. Nobody hit his woman.

Like a raging bull, he bent and plowed into the man closest to him, knocking him off his feet.

The big man fell against the chatty one, and the pair hit the ground, their guns flying from their hands to skitter across the floor, out of their reaches. Rafael rushed toward Caney. "Let her go!"

"Or what?" Caney said, positioning Gisele in front of him like a shield. "You'll shoot?" The ex-con pointed his handgun at Gisele. "Go ahead. See who dies first."

Gisele cried. "Shoot him!"

Rafael stopped, his gun pointed at Caney's chest, which meant he was pointing at Gisele's first. His hand slowly sank. "Don't hurt her."

"Put down your gun," Caney commanded.

Movement out of the corner of Rafael's eye alerted him that one of the men on the floor had untangled himself from the other. He dove for his weapon, rolled onto his back and pointed it at Caney.

Caney's hand jerked around. He fired into the broad chest of Bulldozer One.

Bulldozer Two roared and threw himself at Caney.

Caney fired.

The second big mafia man dropped to the ground and lay still.

"Two down," Caney said. "You want to be next?"

"Shoot him," Gisele begged.

The desperation in her eyes hit Rafael in the heart. If he pulled the trigger and missed, he'd kill Gisele. He couldn't risk it. He couldn't lose her. Not now that he'd found her.

He wanted to wake up every morning with her by his side. To see her pad barefooted in her long skirts, her hair loose around her shoulders. To watch her run her business effectively with care and concern for the happiness of each customer.

He wanted the chance to make her love him like he loved her.

"Shoot him," Gisele said. "He's going to kill you, and then he'll kill me anyway."

"Drop the gun," Caney said. "You don't want her brains splattered across the floor. Do it now."

Rafael lowered his weapon to the ground, moving a little closer as he did. He could take the man down without shooting him if he could get close enough.

"I don't have his money," Gisele said. "I never saw it. Maybe the antique dealer found it before I bought the place. I don't know. Just don't hurt my guy."

"It was in there. You have it, and I want it back," Caney said. "If you don't tell me where it is, I'll make you wish you had. I'll start by shooting your fingers. One at a time." He pressed the barrel of the pistol into her cheek. "Then I'll shoot your toes."

"It won't make a difference," she said. "*I don't know* where your damned money is."

Caney pressed the pistol into her cheek and snarled at Gisele. "You'd better know where it is, or I'll shoot your boyfriend."

"No," Gisele cried, tears streaming down her cheeks. "Don't hurt him. I love him."

"Enough!" a voice said from the hallway.

All eyes turned to the woman wearing a flowing red kaftan, her hair wrapped in a matching scarf. Madam Gautier stood straight, her chin held high. "Release my granddaughter at once, and I will tell you where your money is."

CHAPTER 14

"GRAND-MÈRE!" Gisele cried out as she watched her worst nightmare unfold before her eyes. The lives of the two people she loved most hung by a thread.

"Shush, child," Grand-mère said. "I found da money da day you had da cabinet delivered to my home." She stared down her nose at Caney. "If he wants it, he must release you first."

Caney laughed. "How about we play a little game of chicken with the famous Voodoo queen?" He aimed his gun at Gisele's feet.

Gisele jerked them back as the gun went off. The bullet missed her toes but hit the edge of her sandal.

Caney laughed again. "Next time, I won't miss. So, what's it to be?"

Movement out of the corner of her eye drew Gisele's attention.

With Caney's attention on Grand-mère, Rafael

moved ever so slowly closer to Caney. A few more inches, and he'd be close enough to make a move.

Gisele braced for action.

"I took the money to a safe location," Grand-mère said. "Release my granddaughter, and I will take you there."

"How about I shoot him and take both of you there?" He held Gisele in a necklock as he aimed the gun at Rafael.

No, no, no.

Gisele couldn't wait another second. Caney could pull the trigger like he had on the two mafia men. Taking a deep breath, Gisele relaxed all her muscles and dropped like a deadweight, slipping through Caney's arms toward the floor.

In his struggle to bring her back up, he lowered the barrel of his pistol

Rafael threw himself at Caney.

The gun went off as the three of them landed in a pile on the floor with Gisele trapped beneath them.

The two men rolled to the side, fighting to win. Gisele rolled in the opposite direction and lurched to her feet. The front of her blouse bore a dark red stain.

Blood.

She patted her chest, feeling no pain or wounds, which meant one of the men had sustained a gunshot wound.

Her gut told her it was Rafael. He struggled in his

effort to subdue Caney. The man was a trained Navy SEAL. He should have had Caney under control by now.

Gisele searched the floor for one of the dead men's weapons.

Grand-mère bent beside a chair and lifted a handgun. "Looking for this?"

"Yes!" Gisele took the gun from the older woman and rushed to where Rafael pinned Caney to the floor. She kicked Caney's pistol across the room, out of his reach.

Rafael's breathing came in ragged gasps as if he couldn't get a deep breath. His face was pale.

"I've got him covered," Gisele held the handgun the way Grand-mère had taught her at the gun range, balancing her right hand and the weapon in the palm of her left hand. "Go."

Rafael hesitated. He didn't look like he could hold out much longer.

"I've got him," Gisele said. "I swear I'll shoot his ass if he so much as twitches."

Rafael gave what sounded like a laugh, then coughed. He cocked his arm and punched Caney in the face one last time before he rolled off the man and out of his reach.

Caney lay still, his eyes closed.

"Grand-mère, please call 911," Gisele called out. "We need an ambulance. Now."

Grand-mère already had the landline receiver up to her ear, reporting the attack.

Rafael pushed to his feet, staggered a few steps, then bent and braced his hands on his knees. The front of his shirt had a dark stain that was a little hard to see against the dark fabric.

Gisele monitored his movements out of the corner of her eye while keeping a close eye on Caney.

She studied the man who lay on the floor, eyes closed as if Rafael's last punch had knocked him out. His left arm stretched out beside him, but his right arm was tucked beneath.

Gisele tensed.

In an explosion of motion, Caney sat up and whipped a handgun out from behind him.

Rafael dove for Caney at the same time as Gisele pulled the trigger.

"Oh, sweet peaches!" she yelled and ran to Rafael's side. "Rafael! Please, Rafael, talk to me. Did I shoot you?"

Rafael rocked back and forth as if he was in great pain.

Tears welled in Gisele's eyes. "I'm so sorry. I aimed at Caney. I would never hurt you. Please, please, please be all right. I love you." She wrapped her arms around his back, tears spilling down her cheeks. "Don't be mad at me. I love you, Rafael Romero. It's okay. You don't have to love me back.

You don't have to stay with me. I won't cling. I know you like your freedom. Just please, don't die."

He rocked some more and pulled his arm out from between him and Caney with the other mafia guy's gun dangling from his fingers.

"I'm not going to die," he said weakly. "But I might need help getting up."

Gisele's hands wrapped around one of Rafael's arms. "Is Caney..."

"Dead?" Rafael nodded. "You hit him in the heart. He died instantly."

She let go of a rush of air and put her back into helping Rafael to his feet. "I've never killed a man before," she said softly.

He cupped her cheek with a bloody hand. "Are you okay?"

She nodded. "It was him or you. I chose you. Please, sit before you fall." Gisele wrapped an arm around his waist and guided him to an armchair. "I hear the ambulance coming. We'll get you to the hospital, and they'll fix you up. After all, you said you weren't going to die."

He dropped onto the chair and winced. "Did you mean what you said?"

She couldn't remember anything past Caney sitting up and nearly shooting Rafael. "What did I say?"

"About loving me?"

Her cheeks heated. "Please don't be mad. I love

you, but that doesn't mean you have to love me back. I went into *us* with my eyes wide open. I expect nothing and will take whatever I can get and be fine when you move on."

Grand-mère appeared beside her with a wad of freshly laundered towels. "Apply pressure to da wound so he won't bleed out."

"Right. Yes. You can't bleed out." She laid the towels against the bloody shirt.

He covered her hand with his, moved it to the right position and held it there.

"Before I lose any more blood and pass out, I want to get something clear." His voice was weak.

Gisele choked down a sob and forced a smile. "You should save your strength. I know we made a deal. I'll stand by it."

He raised his other hand and cupped her cheek. "Shush and listen."

She blinked back tears. "Okay."

"I am reneging on that deal. I don't want it anymore."

More tears spilled from her eyes. "Okay. I respect that," she said, a sob rising in her throat. "Well, hell. I promised not to be clingy but cut me a break on a few tears."

He brushed his thumb across her wet cheek. "I want a new deal."

She swallowed hard. "Okay."

"I love you."

Her brow puckered.

He chuckled, coughed and winced. "Hear me out. I love you. I'm glad you love me, and I want you and me to love each other forever. Along with love, I want the 'C' word." He smiled. "I want to commit. I know now that what I felt with my ex-fiancée wasn't love. What I feel with you is something I can't live without. If you need time to think about it and to feel the same, I'll wait. You're worth it."

Gisele blinked at a steady stream of tears. "I don't need time to think about it," she said. "I need you." She started to throw her arms around him but stopped herself, settling for a kiss. She maintained the pressure against his wound until the Emergency Medical Services personnel took over. As they loaded him into the back of the ambulance, her heart swelled with the overwhelming love she felt for the Navy SEAL.

"He's a keeper."

EPILOGUE

Three months later

Rafael stood outside the door to the boat factory, dressed in a black suit and sapphire blue tie and a white rose pinned to his lapel.

Gisele stood beside him, wearing a matching sapphire blue dress that hugged the upper half of her body like a second skin. The skirt flared out from below her hips in billowing drifts of shimmering sapphire chiffon.

She'd worn her hair down in loose, soft curls with a white rose tucked behind her ear, in stark contrast to her dark tresses. She was the most beautiful woman he could ever have dreamed of loving and an even lovelier bride.

Rafael shook his head, aware that he hadn't stopped smiling since he'd woken that morning.

Today was their wedding day.

They'd decided on non-traditional clothing and a non-traditional venue at the boat factory. Gisele had asked Shelby to officiate, even though she was a very plump, eight-month pregnant woman. She was happy, healthy and glad she'd been wrong about Rafael not being the right man for Gisele.

The entire contingent of Bayou Brotherhood Protectors were seated with their women folk.

The music started. Remy and Gerard opened the double doors and stood back for the bride and groom to walk together down the aisle.

Rafael wouldn't have to stand and wait for his bride to come to him. He would be by her side now and forever.

Gisele's friends and her cousin Bianca had decorated the boat factory with lush greenery and white roses.

Rafael had worked with his buddies to arrange a special surprise, bringing Johnny and his cage to the ceremony. The ladies had even decorated his stand.

When Gisele saw the cage, she laughed and squeezed Rafael's hand. "Thank you."

Grand-mère Gautier stood by in a multi-colored kaftan, a serene smile gracing her lips. The day before she'd attended the grand opening of the new women's shelter built with Ronald Caney's bag of money.

As Gisele walked alongside Rafael, she leaned close and whispered, "Did I tell you I'd promised Bianca that I would make you fall in love with me and then dump you to teach you a lesson in love?"

Rafael shot a glance her way, his brow puckered. "Please tell me I'm not about to be pranked."

Gisele laughed. "No. I told her that at least I got it half-right."

"You got me to fall in love with you," he said, squeezing her hand gently. "And you taught me a lesson on love. I'm glad you didn't dump me."

"So am I," Gisele said.

They came to stand in front of Shelby, with Johnny entertaining the crowd with,

You break it, you buy it, asshole.

and

Get me a beer, woman.

As Rafael approached, Johnny had other words to say.

Cheeky Bastard.

and

He's a Keeper.

Rafael knew Gisele had been working with him on a new phrase, but he had yet to hear it.

They read their own vows and promised to love and respect each other. When it came time to say their I dos, Johnny had his two seconds of fame when he added his sentiment…

Just say I do.

Rafael, fully recovered from his wounds, hugged and kissed his wife, happy he'd found the one for him.

BREAKING SILENCE

DELTA FORCE STRONG BOOK #1

New York Times & *USA Today*
Bestselling Author

ELLE JAMES

BREAKING

Silence

DELTA FORCE STRONG

New York Times & USA Today Bestselling Author

ELLE JAMES

CHAPTER 1

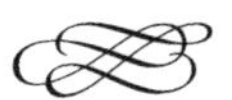

HAD he known they would be deployed so soon after their last short mission to El Salvador, Rucker Sloan wouldn't have bought that dirt bike from his friend Duff. Now, it would sit there for months before he actually got to take it out to the track.

The team had been given forty-eight hours to pack their shit, take care of business and get onto the C130 that would transport them to Afghanistan.

Now, boots on the ground, duffel bags stowed in their assigned quarters behind the wire, they were ready to take on any mission the powers that be saw fit to assign.

What he wanted most that morning, after being awake for the past thirty-six hours, was a cup of strong, black coffee.

The rest of his team had hit the sack as soon as

they got in. Rucker had already met with their commanding officer, gotten a brief introduction to the regional issues and had been told to get some rest. They'd be operational within the next forty-eight hours.

Too wound up to sleep, Rucker followed a stream of people he hoped were heading for the chow hall. He should be able to get coffee there.

On the way, he passed a sand volleyball court where two teams played against each other. One of the teams had four players, the other only three. The four-person squad slammed a ball to the ground on the other side of the net. The only female player ran after it as it rolled toward Rucker.

He stopped the ball with his foot and picked it up.

The woman was tall, slender, blond-haired and blue-eyed. She wore an Army PT uniform of shorts and an Army T-shirt with her hair secured back from her face in a ponytail seated on the crown of her head.

Without makeup, and sporting a sheen of perspiration, she was sexy as hell, and the men on both teams knew it.

They groaned when Rucker handed her the ball. He'd robbed them of watching the female soldier bending over to retrieve the runaway.

She took the ball and frowned. "Do you play?"

"I have," he answered.

"We could use a fourth." She lifted her chin in challenge.

Tired from being awake for the past thirty-six hours, Rucker opened his mouth to say *hell no*. But he made the mistake of looking into her sky-blue eyes and instead said, "I'm in."

What the hell was he thinking?

Well, hadn't he been wound up from too many hours sitting in transit? What he needed was a little physical activity to relax his mind and muscles. At least, that's what he told himself in the split-second it took to step into the sandbox and serve up a heaping helping of whoop-ass.

He served six times before the team playing opposite finally returned one. In between each serve, his side gave him high-fives, all members except one—the blonde with the blue eyes he stood behind, admiring the length of her legs beneath her black Army PT shorts.

Twenty minutes later, Rucker's team won the match. The teams broke up and scattered to get showers or breakfast in the chow hall.

"Can I buy you a cup of coffee?" the pretty blonde asked.

"Only if you tell me your name." He twisted his lips into a wry grin. "I'd like to know who delivered those wicked spikes."

She held out her hand. "Nora Michaels," she said.

He gripped her hand in his, pleased to feel firm pressure. Women might be the weaker sex, but he didn't like a dead fish handshake from males or females. Firm and confident was what he preferred. Like her ass in those shorts.

She cocked an eyebrow. "And you are?"

He'd been so intent thinking about her legs and ass, he'd forgotten to introduce himself. "Rucker Sloan. Just got in less than an hour ago."

"Then you could probably use a tour guide to the nearest coffee."

He nodded. "Running on fumes here. Good coffee will help."

"I don't know about good, but it's coffee and it's fresh." She released his hand and fell in step beside him, heading in the direction of some of the others from their volleyball game.

"As long as it's strong and black, I'll be happy."

She laughed. "And awake for the next twenty-four hours."

"Spoken from experience?" he asked, casting a glance in her direction.

She nodded. "I work nights in the medical facility. It can be really boring and hard to stay awake when we don't have any patients to look after." She held up her hands. "Not that I want any of our boys injured and in need of our care."

"But it does get boring," he guessed.

"It makes for a long deployment." She held out her

hand. "Nice to meet you, Rucker. Is Rucker a call sign or your real name?"

He grinned. "Real name. That was the only thing my father gave me before he cut out and left my mother and me to make it on our own."

"Your mother raised you, and you still joined the Army?" She raised an eyebrow. "Most mothers don't want their boys to go off to war."

"It was that or join a gang and end up dead in a gutter," he said. "She couldn't afford to send me to college. I was headed down the gang path when she gave me the ultimatum. Join and get the GI-Bill, or she would cut me off and I'd be out in the streets. To her, it was the only way to get me out of L.A. and to have the potential to go to college someday."

She smiled "And you stayed in the military."

He nodded. "I found a brotherhood that was better than any gang membership in LA. For now, I take college classes online. It was my mother's dream for me to graduate college. She never went, and she wanted so much more for me than the streets of L.A.. When my gig is up with the Army, if I haven't finished my degree, I'll go to college fulltime."

"And major in what?" Nora asked.

"Business management. I'm going to own my own security service. I want to put my combat skills to use helping people who need dedicated and specialized protection."

Nora nodded. "Sounds like a good plan."

"I know the protection side of things. I need to learn the business side and business law. Life will be different on the civilian side."

"True."

"How about you? What made you sign up?" he asked.

She shrugged. "I wanted to put my nursing degree to good use and help our men and women in uniform. This is my first assignment after training."

"Drinking from the firehose?" Rucker stopped in front of the door to the mess hall.

She nodded. "Yes. But it's the best baptism under fire medical personnel can get. I'll be a better nurse for it when I return to the States."

"How much longer do you have to go?" he asked, hoping that she'd say she'd be there as long as he was. In his case, he never knew how long their deployments would last. One week, one month, six months...

She gave him a lopsided smile. "I ship out in a week."

"That's too bad." He opened the door for her. "I just got here. That doesn't give us much time to get to know each other."

"That's just as well." Nora stepped through the door. "I don't want to be accused of fraternizing. I'm too close to going back to spoil my record."

Rucker chuckled. "Playing volleyball and sharing a table while drinking coffee won't get you written up. I like the way you play. I'm curious to know where you learned to spike like that."

"I guess that's reasonable. Coffee first." She led him into the chow hall.

The smells of food and coffee made Rucker's mouth water.

He grabbed a tray and loaded his plate with eggs, toast and pancakes drenched in syrup. Last, he stopped at the coffee urn and filled his cup with freshly brewed black coffee.

When he looked around, he found Nora seated at one of the tables, holding a mug in her hands, a small plate with cottage cheese and peaches on it.

He strode over to her. "Mind if I join you?"

"As long as you don't hit on me," she said with cocked eyebrows.

"You say that as if you've been hit on before."

She nodded and sipped her steaming brew. "I lost count how many times in the first week I was here."

"Shows they have good taste in women and, unfortunately, limited manners."

"And you're better?" she asked, a smile twitching the corners of her lips.

"I'm not hitting on you. You can tell me to leave, and I'll be out of this chair so fast, you won't have time to enunciate the V."

She stared straight into his eyes, canted her head to one side and said, "Leave."

In the middle of cutting into one of his pancakes,

Rucker dropped his knife and fork on the tray, shot out of his chair and left with his tray, sloshing coffee as he moved. He hoped she was just testing him. If she wasn't…oh, well. He was used to eating meals alone. If she was, she'd have to come to him.

He took a seat at the next table, his back to her, and resumed cutting into his pancake.

Nora didn't utter a word behind him.

Oh, well. He popped a bite of syrupy sweet pancake in his mouth and chewed thoughtfully. She was only there for another week. Man, she had a nice ass…and those legs… He sighed and bent over his plate to stab his fork into a sausage link.

"This chair taken?" a soft, female voice sounded in front of him.

He looked up to see the pretty blond nurse standing there with her tray in her hands, a crooked smile on her face.

He lifted his chin in silent acknowledgement.

She laid her tray on the table and settled onto the chair. "I didn't think you'd do it."

"Fair enough. You don't know me," he said.

"I know that you joined the Army to get out of street life. That your mother raised you after your father skipped out, that you're working toward a business degree and that your name is Rucker." She sipped her coffee.

He nodded, secretly pleased she'd remembered all

that. Maybe there was hope for getting to know the pretty nurse before she redeployed to the States. And who knew? They might run into each other on the other side of the pond.

Still, he couldn't show too much interest, or he'd be no better than the other guys who'd hit on her. "Since you're redeploying back to the States in a week, and I'm due to go out on a mission, probably within the next twenty-four to forty-eight hours, I don't know if it's worth our time to get to know each other any more than we already have."

She nodded. "I guess that's why I want to sit with you. You're not a danger to my perfect record of no fraternizing. I don't have to worry that you'll fall in love with me in such a short amount of time." She winked.

He chuckled. "As I'm sure half of this base has fallen in love with you since you've been here."

She shrugged. "I don't know if it's love, but it's damned annoying."

"How so?"

She rolled her eyes toward the ceiling. "I get flowers left on my door every day."

"And that's annoying? I'm sure it's not easy coming up with flowers out here in the desert." He set down his fork and took up his coffee mug. "I think it's sweet." He held back a smile. Well, almost.

"They're hand-drawn on notepad paper and left

on the door of my quarters and on the door to the shower tent." She shook her head. "It's kind of creepy and stalkerish."

Rucker nodded. "I see your point. The guys should at least have tried their hands at origami flowers, since the real things are scarce around here."

Nora smiled. "I'm not worried about the pictures, but the line for sick call is ridiculous."

"How so?"

"So many of the guys come up with the lamest excuses to come in and hit on me. I asked to work the nightshift to avoid sick call altogether."

"You have a fan group." He smiled. "Has the adoration gone to your head?"

She snorted softly. "No."

"You didn't get this kind of reaction back in the States?"

"I haven't been on active duty for long. I only decided to join the Army after my mother passed away. I was her fulltime nurse for a couple years as she went through stage four breast cancer. We thought she might make it." Her shoulders sagged. "But she didn't."

"I'm sorry to hear that. My mother meant a lot to me, as well. I sent money home every month after I enlisted and kept sending it up until the day she died suddenly of an aneurysm."

"I'm so sorry about your mother's passing," Nora

said, shaking her head. "Wow. As an enlisted man, how did you make enough to send some home?"

"I ate in the chow hall and lived on post. I didn't party or spend money on civilian clothes or booze. Mom needed it. I gave it to her."

"You were a good son to her," Nora said.

His chest tightened. "She died of an aneurysm a couple of weeks before she was due to move to Texas where I'd purchased a house for her."

"Wow. And, let me guess, you blame yourself for not getting her to Texas sooner…?" Her gaze captured his.

Her words hit home, and he winced. "Yeah. I should've done it sooner."

"Can't bring people back with regrets." Nora stared into her coffee cup. "I learned that. The only thing I could do was move forward and get on with living. I wanted to get away from Milwaukee and the home I'd shared with my mother. Not knowing where else to go, I wandered past a realtor's office and stepped into a recruiter's office. I had my nursing degree, they wanted and needed nurses on active duty. I signed up, they put me through some officer training and here I am." She held her arms out.

"Playing volleyball in Afghanistan, working on your tan during the day and helping soldiers at night." Rucker gave her a brief smile. "I, for one, appreciate what you're doing for our guys and gals."

"I do the best I can," she said softly. "I just wish I

could do more. I'd rather stay here than redeploy back to the States, but they're afraid if they keep us here too long, we'll burn out or get PTSD."

"One week, huh?"

She nodded. "One week."

"In my field, one week to redeploy back to the States is a dangerous time. Anything can happen and usually does."

"Yeah, but you guys are on the frontlines, if not behind enemy lines. I'm back here. What could happen?"

Rucker flinched. "Oh, sweetheart, you didn't just say that..." He glanced around, hoping no one heard her tempt fate with those dreaded words *What could happen?*

Nora grinned. "You're not superstitious, are you?"

"In what we do, we can't afford not to be," he said, tossing salt over his shoulder.

"I'll be fine," she said in a reassuring, nurse's voice.

"Stop," he said, holding up his hand. "You're only digging the hole deeper." He tossed more salt over his other shoulder.

Nora laughed.

"Don't laugh." He handed her the saltshaker. "Do it."

"I'm not tossing salt over my shoulder. Someone has to clean the mess hall."

Rucker leaned close and shook salt over her shoulder. "I don't know if it counts if someone else throws salt over your shoulder, but I figure you now need every bit of luck you can get."

"You're a fighter but afraid of a little bad luck." Nora shook her head. "Those two things don't seem to go together."

"You'd be surprised how easily my guys are freaked by the littlest things."

"And you," she reminded him.

"You asking *what could happen?* isn't a little thing. That's in-your-face tempting fate." Rucker was laying it on thick to keep her grinning, but deep down, he believed what he was saying. And it didn't make a difference the amount of education he had or the statistics that predicted outcomes. His gut told him she'd just tempted fate with her statement. Maybe he was overthinking things. Now, he was worried she wouldn't make it back to the States alive.

NORA LIKED RUCKER. He was the first guy who'd walked away without an argument since she'd arrived at the base in Afghanistan. He'd meant what he'd said and proved it. His dark brown hair and deep green eyes, coupled with broad shoulders and a narrow waist, made him even more attractive. Not all the men were in as good a shape as Rucker. And he seemed to have a very determined attitude.

She hadn't known what to expect when she'd

deployed. Being the center of attention of almost every single male on the base hadn't been one of her expectations. She'd only ever considered herself average in the looks department. But when the men outnumbered women by more than ten to one, she guessed average appearance moved up in the ranks.

"Where did you learn to play volleyball?" Rucker asked, changing the subject of her leaving and her flippant comment about what could happen in one week.

"I was on the volleyball team in high school. It got me a scholarship to a small university in my home state of Minnesota, where I got my Bachelor of Science degree in Nursing."

"It takes someone special to be a nurse," he stated. "Is that what you always wanted to be?"

She shook her head. "I wanted to be a firefighter when I was in high school."

"What made you change your mind?"

She stared down at the coffee growing cold in her mug. "My mother was diagnosed with cancer when I was a senior in high school. I wanted to help but felt like I didn't know enough to be of assistance." She looked up. "She made it through chemo and radiation treatments and still came to all of my volleyball games. I thought she was in the clear."

"She wasn't?" Rucker asked, his tone low and gentle.

"She didn't tell me any different. When I got the

scholarship, I told her I wanted to stay close to home to be with her. She insisted I go and play volleyball for the university. I was pretty good and played for the first two years I was there. I quit the team in my third year to start the nursing program. I didn't know there was anything wrong back home. I called every week to talk to Mom. She never let on that she was sick." She forced a smile. "But you don't want my sob story. You probably want to know what's going on around here."

He set his mug on the table. "If we were alone in a coffee bar back in the States, I'd reach across the table and take your hand."

"Oh, please. Don't do that." She looked around the mess hall, half expecting someone might have overheard Rucker's comment. "You're enlisted. I'm an officer. That would get us into a whole lot of trouble."

"Yeah, but we're also two human beings. I wouldn't be human if I didn't feel empathy for you and want to provide comfort."

She set her coffee cup on the table and laid her hands in her lap. "I'll be satisfied with the thought. Thank you."

"Doesn't seem like enough. When did you find out your mother was sick?"

She swallowed the sadness that welled in her throat every time she remembered coming home to find out her mother had been keeping her illness from her. "It wasn't until I went home for Christmas in my senior year that I realized she'd been lying to me for a while." She laughed in lieu of sobbing. "I don't care who they are, old people don't always tell the truth."

"How long had she been keeping her sickness from you?"

"She'd known the cancer had returned halfway through my junior year. I hadn't gone home that summer because I'd been working hard to get my coursework and clinical hours in the nursing program. When I went home at Christmas..." Nora gulped. "She wasn't the same person. She'd lost so much weight and looked twenty years older."

"Did you stay home that last semester?" Rucker asked.

"Mom insisted I go back to school and finish what I'd started. Like your mother, she hadn't gone to college. She wanted her only child to graduate. She was afraid that if I stayed home to take care of her, I wouldn't finish my nursing degree."

"I heard from a buddy of mine that those programs can be hard to get into," he said. "I can see why she wouldn't want you to drop everything in your life to take care of her."

Nora gave him a watery smile. "That's what she said. As soon as my last final was over, I returned to my hometown. I became her nurse. She lasted another three months before she slipped away."

"That's when you joined the Army?"

She shook her head. "Dad was so heartbroken, I stayed a few months until he was feeling better. I got a job at a local emergency room. On weekends, my father and I worked on cleaning out the house and getting it ready to put on the market."

"Is your dad still alive?" Rucker asked.

Nora nodded. "He lives in Texas. He moved to a small house with a big backyard." She forced a smile. "He has a garden, and all the ladies in his retirement community think he's the cat's meow. He still misses Mom, but he's getting on with his life."

Rucker tilted his head. "When did you join the military?"

"When Dad sold the house and moved into his retirement community. I worried about him, but he's doing better."

"And you?"

"I miss her. But she'd whip my ass if I wallowed in self-pity for more than a moment. She was a strong woman and expected me to be the same."

Rucker grinned. "From what I've seen, you are."

Nora gave him a skeptical look. "You've only seen me playing volleyball. It's just a game." Not that she'd admit it, but she was a real softy when it came to caring for the sick and injured.

"If you're half as good at nursing, which I'm willing to bet you are, you're amazing." He started to reach across the table for her hand. Before he actually touched her, he grabbed the saltshaker and shook it over his cold breakfast.

"You just got in this morning?" Nora asked.

Rucker nodded.

"How long will you be here?" she asked.

"I don't know."

"What do you mean, you don't know? I thought when people were deployed, they were given a specific timeframe."

"Most people are. We're deployed where and when needed."

Nora frowned. "What are you? Some kind of special forces team?"

His lips pressed together. "Can't say."

She sat back. He was some kind of Special Forces. "Army, right?"

He nodded.

That would make him Delta Force. The elite of the elite. A very skilled soldier who undertook incredibly dangerous missions. She gulped and stopped herself from reaching across the table to take his hand. "Well, I hope all goes well while you and your team are here."

"Thanks."

A man hurried across the chow hall wearing shorts and an Army T-shirt. He headed directly toward their table.

Nora didn't recognize him. "Expecting someone?" she asked Rucker, tipping her head toward the man.

Rucker turned, a frown pulling his eyebrows together. "Why the hell's Dash awake?"

Nora frowned. "Dash? Please tell me that's his callsign, not his real name."

Rucker laughed. "It should be his real name. He's first into the fight, and he's fast." Rucker stood and faced his teammate. "What's up?"

"CO wants us all in the Tactical Operations Center," Dash said. "On the double."

"Guess that's my cue to exit." Rucker turned to Nora. "I enjoyed our talk."

She nodded. "Me, too."

Dash grinned. "Tell you what…I'll stay and finish your conversation while you see what the commander wants."

Rucker hooked Dash's arm twisted it up behind his back, and gave him a shove toward the door. "You heard the CO, he wants all of us." Rucker winked at Nora. "I hope to see you on the volleyball court before you leave."

"Same. Good luck." Nora's gaze followed Rucker's broad shoulders and tight ass out of the chow hall. Too bad she'd only be there another week before she shipped out. She would've enjoyed more volleyball and coffee with the Delta Force operative.

He'd probably be on maneuvers that entire week.

She stacked her tray and coffee cup in the collection area and left the chow hall, heading for the building where she shared her quarters with Beth

Drennan, a nurse she'd become friends with during their deployment together.

As close as they were, Nora didn't bring up her conversation with the Delta. With only a week left at the base, she probably wouldn't run into him again. Though she would like to see him again, she prayed he didn't end up in the hospital.

ABOUT THE AUTHOR

ELLE JAMES also writing as MYLA JACKSON is a *New York Times* and *USA Today* Bestselling author of books including cowboys, intrigues and paranormal adventures that keep her readers on the edges of their seats. When she's not at her computer, she's traveling, snow skiing, boating, or riding her ATV, dreaming up new stories. Learn more about Elle James at www.ellejames.com

Website | Facebook | Twitter | GoodReads | Newsletter | BookBub | Amazon

Or visit her alter ego Myla Jackson at mylajackson.com
Website | Facebook | Twitter | Newsletter

Follow Me!
www.ellejames.com
ellejamesauthor@gmail.com

ALSO BY ELLE JAMES

A Killer Series

Chilled (#1)

Scorched (#2)

Erased (#3)

Swarmed (#4)

Brotherhood Protectors International

Athens Affair (#1)

Belgian Betrayal (#2)

Croatia Collateral (#3)

Dublin Debacle (#4)

Edinburgh Escape (#5)

Frankfurt Fallout (#6)

Brotherhood Protectors Hawaii

Kalea's Hero (#1)

Leilani's Hero (#2)

Kiana's Hero (#3)

Maliea's Hero (#4)

Emi's Hero (#5)

Sachie's Hero (#6)

Bayou Brotherhood Protectors

Remy (#1)

Gerard (#2)

Lucas (#3)

Beau (#4)

Rafael (#5)

Valentin (#6)

Landry (#7)

Simon (#8)

Maurice (#9)

Jacques (#10)

Brotherhood Protectors Yellowstone

Saving Kyla (#1)

Saving Chelsea (#2)

Saving Amanda (#3)

Saving Liliana (#4)

Saving Breely (#5)

Saving Savvie (#6)

Saving Jenna (#7)

Saving Peyton (#8)

Saving Londyn (#9)

Brotherhood Protectors Colorado

SEAL Salvation (#1)

Rocky Mountain Rescue (#2)

Ranger Redemption (#3)

Tactical Takeover (#4)

Colorado Conspiracy (#5)

Rocky Mountain Madness (#6)

Free Fall (#7)

Colorado Cold Case (#8)

Fool's Folly (#9)

Colorado Free Rein (#10)

Rocky Mountain Venom (#11)

High Country Hero (#12)

Brotherhood Protectors

Montana SEAL (#1)

Bride Protector SEAL (#2)

Montana D-Force (#3)

Cowboy D-Force (#4)

Montana Ranger (#5)

Montana Dog Soldier (#6)

Montana SEAL Daddy (#7)

Montana Ranger's Wedding Vow (#8)

Montana SEAL Undercover Daddy (#9)

Cape Cod SEAL Rescue (#10)

Montana SEAL Friendly Fire (#11)

Montana SEAL's Mail-Order Bride (#12)

SEAL Justice (#13)

Ranger Creed (#14)

Delta Force Rescue (#15)

Dog Days of Christmas (#16)

Montana Rescue (#17)

Montana Ranger Returns (#18)

Brotherhood Protectors Boxed Set 1

Brotherhood Protectors Boxed Set 2

Brotherhood Protectors Boxed Set 3

Brotherhood Protectors Boxed Set 4

Brotherhood Protectors Boxed Set 5

Brotherhood Protectors Boxed Set 6

Iron Horse Legacy

Soldier's Duty (#1)

Ranger's Baby (#2)

Marine's Promise (#3)

SEAL's Vow (#4)

Warrior's Resolve (#5)

Drake (#6)

Grimm (#7)

Murdock (#8)

Utah (#9)

Judge (#10)

Delta Force Strong

Ivy's Delta (Delta Force 3 Crossover)

Breaking Silence (#1)

Breaking Rules (#2)

Breaking Away (#3)

Breaking Free (#4)

Breaking Hearts (#5)

Breaking Ties (#6)

Breaking Point (#7)

Breaking Dawn (#8)

Breaking Promises (#9)

Hearts & Heroes Series

Wyatt's War (#1)

Mack's Witness (#2)

Ronin's Return (#3)

Sam's Surrender (#4)

Hellfire Series

Hellfire, Texas (#1)

Justice Burning (#2)

Smoldering Desire (#3)

Hellfire in High Heels (#4)

Playing With Fire (#5)

Up in Flames (#6)

Total Meltdown (#7)

Take No Prisoners Series

SEAL's Honor (#1)

SEAL'S Desire (#2)

SEAL's Embrace (#3)

SEAL's Obsession (#4)

SEAL's Proposal (#5)

SEAL's Seduction (#6)

SEAL'S Defiance (#7)

SEAL's Deception (#8)

SEAL's Deliverance (#9)

SEAL's Ultimate Challenge (#10)

Texas Billionaire Club

Tarzan & Janine (#1)

Something To Talk About (#2)

Who's Your Daddy (#3)

Love & War (#4)

Billionaire Online Dating Service

The Billionaire Husband Test (#1)

The Billionaire Cinderella Test (#2)

The Billionaire Bride Test (#3)

The Billionaire Daddy Test (#4)

The Billionaire Matchmaker Test (#5)

The Billionaire Glitch Date (#6)

The Billionaire Perfect Date (#7)

The Billionaire Replacement Date (#8)

The Billionaire Wedding Date (#9)

Cajun Magic Mystery Series

Voodoo on the Bayou (#1)

Voodoo for Two (#2)

Deja Voodoo (#3)

Damned if You Voodoo (#4)

Voodoo or Die (#5)

The Outriders

Homicide at Whiskey Gulch (#1)

Hideout at Whiskey Gulch (#2)

Held Hostage at Whiskey Gulch (#3)

Setup at Whiskey Gulch (#4)

Missing Witness at Whiskey Gulch (#5)

Cowboy Justice at Whiskey Gulch (#6)

Boys Behaving Badly Anthologies

Rogues (#1)

Blue Collar (#2)

Pirates (#3)

Stranded (#4)

First Responder (#5)

Cowboys (#6)

Silver Soldiers (#7)

Secret Identities (#8)

Warrior's Conquest

Enslaved by the Viking Short Story

Conquests

Smokin' Hot Firemen

Protecting the Colton Bride

Protecting the Colton Bride & Colton's Cowboy Code

Heir to Murder

Secret Service Rescue

High Octane Heroes

Haunted

Engaged with the Boss

Cowboy Brigade

An Unexpected Clue

Under Suspicion, With Child

Texas-Size Secrets

Made in the USA
Middletown, DE
14 December 2024